ASSASSIN

Cover design by David Stockman

Also by Brian Nicholson featuring John Gunn

GWEILO

AL SAMAK

ASHANTI GOLD

FIRE DRAGON

CALYPSO

SHARK

TRAITOR

ASSASSIN

BRIAN NICHOLSON

TRAFFORD PUBLISHING

Order this book on line at www.trafford.com/
or email orders@trafford.com

Most Trafford titles are also available at major online book retailers.

© Copyright 2012 Brian Nicholson
All rights reserved. No part of this publication may be reproduced, stored in a retrieval system, or transmitted, in any form or by any means, electronic, mechanical, photocopying, recording, or otherwise, without the written prior permission of the author.

This book is a work of fiction and all the characters, places and events in this book are fictitious, and any resemblance to actual persons, living or dead, is purely coincidental.

Note for Librarians: A cataloguing record for this book is available from Library and Archives Canada at www.collectionscanada.ca/amicus/index-e.html
Printed in the United States of America

ISBN: 978-1-4669-2935-7 (sc)
ISBN: 978-1-4669-2934-0 (hc)
ISBN: 978-1-4669-2933-3 (e)

Library of Congress Control Number: 2012906492

Trafford rev. 04/10/2012

www.trafford.com
North America and International
toll-free: 1 888 232 4444 (USA & Canada)
phone: 250 363 6864 + fax: 812 355 4082

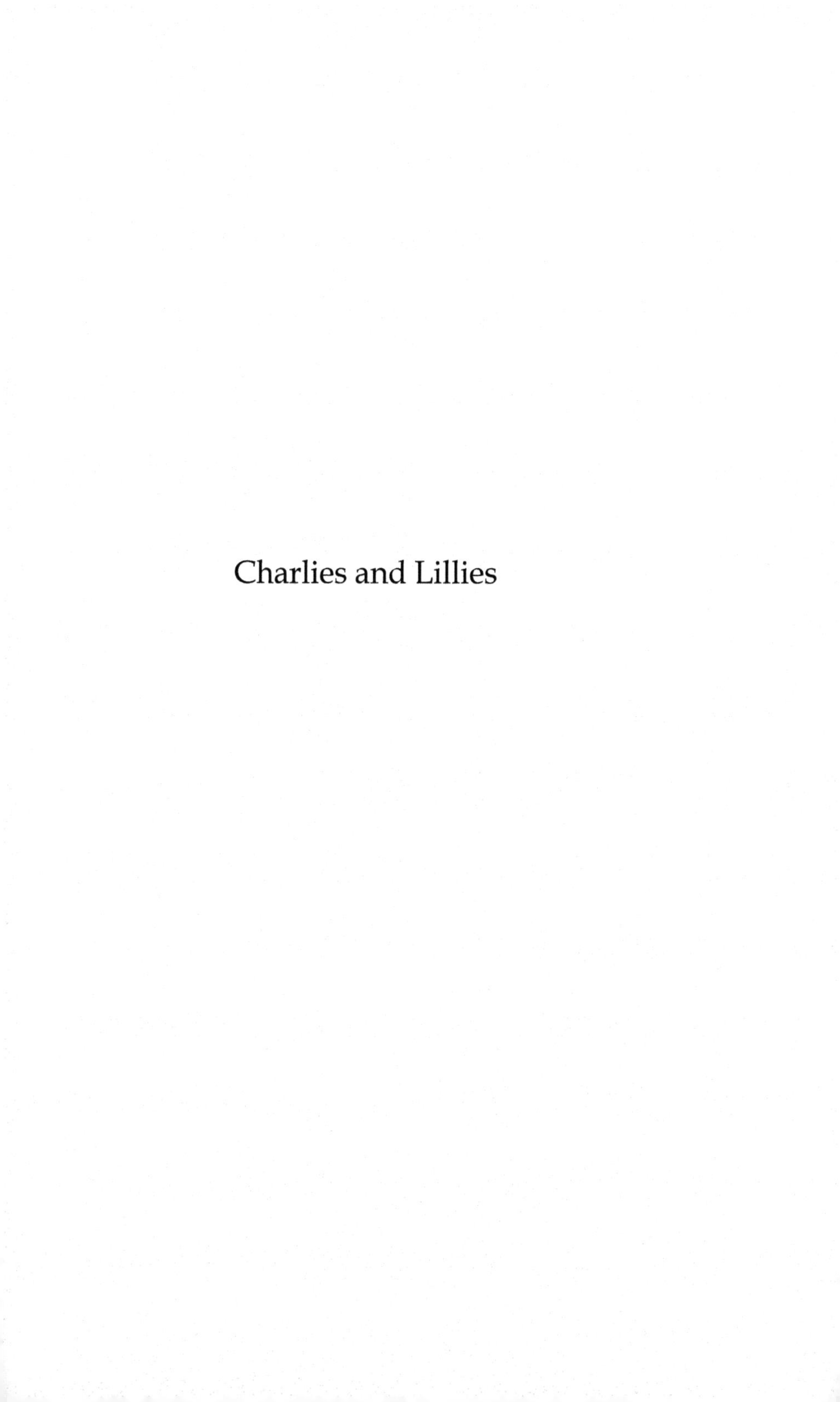

Charlies and Lillies

FOREWORD

In 1988, after a series of leaks and defections in MI5 and MI6, the Prime Minister tasked a relatively young Major General, who had retired at the age of 48, with the reorganisation of the United Kingdom's Intelligence Services. After retirement he had redirected his talents into management consultancy and turned two failing companies from near bankruptcy to healthy, profit-making concerns.

Within a year of being given the remit to set up an effective, efficient and secure intelligence service, he had created the British Intelligence Directorate. Both the espionage and counter-espionage departments were brought under the same roof where their efforts were complimentary rather than contradictory. Very few MI5 and MI6 personnel survived the stringent security vetting initiated by the new director. The two buildings at Millbank and Vauxhall Cross were retained, but only for a limited period during the changeover, as an overt intelligence front. In reality they had little more than a clerical role for storage and retrieval of historical intelligence material.

Kingsroad House was purpose-built for BID in Cale Street to the north of the King's Road. Outwardly it claimed to be the head office of Express Delivery Services (EDS). Access to EDS was by the main entrance on Cale Street while access to BID was either via the main entrance or via the 10th floor of the adjacent multi-storey NCP car park. There were two other headquarter buildings; one in Kingston-on-Thames and another in Southampton. Both had a similar layout to Kingsroad House, but possessed subtle variations in case security was compromised.

Kingsroad House had fourteen above-ground floors, with a helipad on the fifteenth floor. There were three basement levels, which contained BID's emergency medical centre - the main medical facility was at Maidenhead - an extensive transport department, stores, a small armoury and a weapns testing area. The lowest basement level also provided access to four passages that could be used by BID staff to leave the building avoiding any form of surveillance.

BID became operational in April 1990.

PROLOGUE

On 1st September 1983, Korean Air lines Boeing 747-230BHL 7442 Flight 007, from John F Kennedy International Airport in New York to Gimpo International Airport in South Korea via Anchorage in Alaska, was shot down by a Soviet Sukhoi SU-15 'Flagon' interceptor. The Boeing 747 had strayed into Soviet airspace south of the Kamchatka Peninsula over the Sea of Japan above Moneron Island and to the west of Sakhalin Island.

This incident took place at the height of the Cold War when President Reagan had declared that the Soviet Union was the 'Evil Empire'. Also at this time the USA was implementing its Strategic Defence Initiative with the deployment in Europe of Pershing II missiles, encircling the Soviet Union. As a result of this incident Ronald Reagan directed the US Military to make the US-controlled Global Positioning System (GPS) available for civilian use to prevent another navigational error such as that of KAL Flight 007.

At this time of heightened tension between the USA and USSR, the General Secretary of the Soviet Union was the hard-line, ex-KGB Director, Yuri Andropov who denied that any such incident had occurred. In hindsight, it is possible that the inept handling of the political events by the Soviet Union at this time was due to the failing health of Andropov who was permanently hospitalised by the end of September 1983.

It was only after the collapse of the Soviet Union in 1991 that Boris Yeltsin, on a goodwill visit to Seoul in November 1992, handed over the Flight Data Recorder (FDR) and the Cockpit Voice Recorder (CVR) of Flight 007. This confirmed that the Soviet Union had known of the crash site of KAL Flight 007 since 1st September 1983.

The Soviet Union reported that all 269 passengers and crew of Flight KAL 007 were killed when the Boeing 747 ditched into the sea near Sakhalin Island.

FARAWAY TRAVEL

From 15th to 30th May 2011, Faraway Travel Ltd, whose company logo was a globe within an oyster shell and the slogan, 'We make the World your oyster', was offering the following package discovery tour:

Day 1 *Fly to Moscow*
Stay night in Courtyard Marriot
Day 2 *Fly to Irkutsk*
Stay 2 nights in Hotel Courtyard Irkutsk
Day 5 *Boat on Lake Baikal to Severobajkalsk*
2 days in Hotel Baikal at Severobajkalsk
Day 8 *BAM railway to Vladivostok via:*
Tynda, Komsomolsk, Sovelskaya and Khabarovsk - 3 Days
Day 12 *Vladivostok*
2 Nights at Vladivostok Hotel
Day 14 *Fly to Moscow*
Stay night at Courtyard Marriot
Day 15 *Fly to London*

Eight people had signed up for this package discovery tour:

Mr and Mrs Woodford from Manchester, UK
Mrs Myra Hurst from Indianapolis, Indiana, USA
Mrs Agnetha Hensen from Stockholm, Sweden
Miss Lucy Brahms from London, UK
Miss Rachel Groves from London, UK
Mr Martin Baldwin from Chelmsford, UK
Mr Peter van den Platt from Brussels, Belgium

CHAPTER 1

'Holy shit!...what motherfuck....' but before the young patrol officer could finish his expletive and reach the washroom, he retched violently and his vomit joined that of the victim's blood, urine, faeces and vomit. 'Jeeeeezus,' he mumbled clearing the vomit and saliva from his mouth with a tissue as he fumbled for his radio. 'I'm at North Park Road off East Sheffield Drive,' a pause as the Police Department at East 3rd Street in the city centre of Indianapolis responded. 'What number?...er...er...wait,' as he back-tracked to the open front door which had a brass '1' on it. 'That's number one....a homicide....woman's been murdered.'

Screaming sirens preceded the arrival of two cars from the Indianapolis Metropolitan Police Department Homicide Squad together with the PD's forensic team. A small group of neighbours and the inevitable voyeurs had gathered on the front lawn of 1 North Park Road. These were quickly moved on except for Mr and Mrs Wilson from 3 North Park Road.

Lt McLeod was the IMPD's detective from Homicide who was first on the crime scene. After twenty-two years in the PD, even he had to breathe through his mouth to avoid the involuntary reaction of retching. He turned to the young patrol officer who had followed him.

'Harris....isn't it?'

'Yes sir.'

'First homicide?'

'Yes sir.'

'Who called this in?'

'The Wilsons......from number 3. They hadn't seen this...er...this woman...er...Mrs Hurst,' the officer corrected, checking the name he'd written in his notebook when he'd arrived to be met by the Wilsons. 'They hadn't seen her for two days.'

'Any of this yours, son?' McLeod waved a hand at the blood and vomit surrounding the armchair in which the naked body of the woman had been restrained with a rope around her torso.

'Yes sir.......there.....I didn't make it....'

'Forget it son. I tossed my cookies at my first homicide. You come with me while I speak to the Wilsons. Forensics!' McLeod turned to the white-overalled team. 'Crime scene's all yours.'

The scene was horrific. Mrs Hurst, a woman in her late fifties or early sixties had been stripped naked and tied round the top of her torso into an armchair. How long the torture had lasted before she died would be a matter for forensics, but to even the untrained eye her mutilation was all too obvious and horrific. During the torture the poor woman had fouled herself on several occasions adding degrading humiliation to the appalling pain she must have suffered.

Dreadful burns showed that electric terminals had been attached to her breasts and genitals and nails had been wrenched from several fingers. She'd finally been beheaded. The severed head lay on the floor amongst the vomit and faeces, the sightless eyes staring up at the ceiling.

McLeod took a deep breath of fresh air as he and Officer Harris walked out from the house onto the lawn to meet the neighbours who had dialled 911 when they got no response to ringing the bell on number one.

'Mr and Mrs Wilson?'

'Yes officer.'

'I'm Lieutenant McLeod and this is Officer Harris who you've met already. McLeod held up his badge for the Wilsons to see. 'What can you tell me about Mrs Hurst?'

'We've known Myra....and her husband Jim, for more'n sixteen years since they moved in. Jim died of a heart attack three years gone.'

'Mrs Hurst has been murdered.....'

'No!' Mrs Wilson gasped.

'Why would anyone want to murder her? Did she keep money in the house or.....'

'No....no....nothing like that. Jim left Myra with a comfortable income so she could take a vacation each year.'

'When was that?'

'Just last month...no wait...we're July now. It was the last two weeks of May.'

'And where did she go?'

'Russia.'

'Russia? Why there?'

'Both Myra and Jim had always been interested in Russia. They used to take a holiday there every year in one part or another of the country. That was interrupted when Jim died. We thought she went on the vacation as a sort of memorial to Jim.' All of this information was coming from Mrs Wilson. Her husband had barely spoken a word during the questioning.

'I guess we'll find details of the vacation when we search the house, but can you remember what travel agent she used Mrs Wilson?'

'Oh yes, we spent many evenings discussing her itinerary with her. It was the same travel agent each year. Now let me think....something to do with far-off places.....no...er.....'

'Faraway Travel,' was offered by Mr Wilson, the first and only time that he had spoken.

CHAPTER 2

'Harris!' McLeod's shout halted the patrol officer who was making his way back to his car.

'Yes sir.'

'You can join Sergeant Ballard and the other officers in the homicide squad searching the house now that forensics have finished.' This was prompted by the emergence from 1 North Park Road of a body bag containing the body of Mrs Hurst followed by the pathologist and a CSI with a plastic bag containing her head.

'I'd better check.....'

'Don't you worry son about checking with traffic. I'll clear it with your Lieutenant Ramsden.' Harris made his way, reluctantly, towards the group of officers who had gathered round McLeod on the lawn.

'Right listen up. Whoever tortured and killed this woman had searched the house pretty carefully first. You'll see signs of that when we get in there. So what are we looking for? I guess two things; first, any documents, letters, brochures or whatever relating to Faraway Travel.' McLeod saw that Harris was writing in his notebook. 'Second, whatever it was that the murderer tried to find, but failed........yes Harris?' The traffic officer had raised his hand.

'How do you know he didn't find what he was looking for sir?'

'No don't make fun of the lad,' McLeod admonished the other officers in his squad who showed amusement at the young officer's interruption. 'The question is valid. If the murderer had found what he was looking for then he would have killed the lady and gone. Since her neighbours have told me that Mrs Hurst had no money or valuable jewellery in the house and the only thing she'd ever done out of the ordinary was to go on vacations in Russia, I believe that she may have been given something or had something put in her pocket or luggage by someone in Russia. I don't think she even knew that she had it........whatever it is......was. I'm certain that if she'd known what it was she would have handed it over at the first threat of torture. OK, any questions now?' There were none and the four officers including Harris entered the house followed by McLeod.

Every corner of the house was searched including the attic and the small basement containing the heating system and laundry. Every item relating to the holiday in Russia including a photo album, digital camera and all the documents and correspondence relating to the holiday were bagged up. The carpet was lifted, but there was no sign of anything that could have warranted the sadistic torture of a middle-aged woman to hand it over. The homicide squad gathered in the hall of 1 North Park Road with plastic bags containing everything that might shed any light on the gruesome death of Mrs Hurst.

'Where's Officer Harris?' McLeod asked

'I'll check,' this from Sgt Ballard who went back into the room where Mrs Hurst had been found. Harris was bent over a glass-fronted bookcase studying a collection of music CDs.

'C'mon Harris, we've been through that bookcase.'

'Yes, I know Sarge' but there's something odd here.'

'What've you found that we all missed?'

'Not sure it's anything, but all these CDs are recordings of light music. Sort of background music like you hear at a party or in a hotel lobby.'

'And?'

'Except this one,' and Harris held up a CD. This is the opera 'Prince Igor' by the Russian composer Alexander Borodin.'

CHAPTER 3

'OK Mac, so what's so special about that CD?' The question came from Charles Clifford, the Chief of the Indianapolis Metropolitan Police Department. Having examined the CD, Lt 'Mac' McLeod had been told by the Captain in charge of the IMPD Homicide Department to take it to the Chief. The Chief looked up from the pile of papers on his desk and removed his reading glasses.

'I'm no classical music buff,' McLeod answered, but the sooner that gets into the hands of the Feds or the spooks in Virginia the better.'

'Why's that?' Chief Clifford asked examining the CD, which was inside its plastic evidence bag.

'I'm told that the opera 'Prince Igor' was written by this Russian guy, Borodin, but he died before he finished it. Two other guys, Rimsky-Korsakov and another guy whose name I've forgotten - Glaznoff or something like that - finished it. It's in four acts and when played, the prologue or overture or whatever comes over fine, but then it stops and this guy starts talking about that Korean Boeing 747 which the Soviets shot down back in 1983.'

'You've listened to all of it?'

'No sir, but enough to understand why Mrs Hurst's murderer was so desperate to find what had been given to her during her package tour to Vladivostok.'

'And that was, Mac?'

'According to this guy on the CD, it seems the 747 never crashed or if it did all the passengers and crew survived.

They were sent to various remote gulags where they were committed to a life sentence of various forms of slave labour.'

'We know that's what's been going on in the Soviet Union for years and not much has changed since Gorbachev and Yeltsin brought an end to the Union. So what's with the desperation and depraved torture to find the CD Mac?'

'It seems this guy - a passenger on the 747 - has escaped from a gulag. The guy's Korean - a scientist - and has been working on some very advanced fuel-cell research. He's trying to get to the West.'

'Aaaah! That might explain the sadistic torture and murder of Mrs Hurst. I'll take it from here Mac.'

As Lt 'Mac' McLeod left the Chief's office, the latter picked up his phone and dialled a number which rang in an office at 575 North Pennsylvania Street in Indianapolis.

'FBI, Special Agent in Charge, Michael Scott.'

'Michael, Chief Clifford, spare me a few minutes right now?'

'Of course Chief.'

'Be with you in ten minutes.'

From Indianapolis the CD was flown to the FBI Headquarters at 935 Pennsylvania Avenue in Washington where it arrived on the desk of the FBI Director, Robert Mueller. It then went by helicopter to the CIA Headquarters at Langley in Virginia where it landed on the desk of the Head of the National Clandestine Service, Patrick Merton. There were three other directorates in the CIA, all of which carried Deputy Director status. These were Intelligence, Support and Science and Technology. Mark Cavendish, the Deputy Director of the latter was sitting in a chair opposite Patrick Merton's desk.

'From your phone call I see we're back on that old chestnut of Korean Airlines Flight 007.........Christ! There must be more conspiracy theories than there were passengers on that airplane. Mind if I help myself to coffee?'

'Help yourself. This take on that blundering tragedy of the Soviet era is just slightly different. See what you think,' and so saying he pressed the 'play' button on the CD player. The message was in word-perfect English with only the slightest trace of a Slavic accent.

'If you are listening to this then I am probably dead as it was my intention to bring it to Langley myself. Who I am is irrelevant. I hope that this recording has reached the USA as I identified that Mrs Hurst was the only US citizen on the Faraway Travel package tour.'

'You will be familiar with the countless conspiracy theories about what happened to KAL Flight 007 when it was shot down on September 1 1983 so I have no intention of repeating all the ridiculous efforts made by the Soviet Union to deceive the USA, Koreans and the rest of the World.'

'The Boeing 747 was hit by two missiles which caused it it to depressurize, but not one of the engines was disabled. The crew of the Boeing was able to ditch it in the sea near Moneron Island from where all the crew and passengers were taken to the KGB Coastguard base on Sakhalin Island. Within a few days everyone was taken to the KGB base at Sovetskaya Gavan in Siberia opposite Sakhalin Island, 600 miles north of Vladivostok. Here the men, women and children were divided into separate groups. The men and women were taken by train to Tynda on the Baikal-Amur Mainline Railway about 800 miles further inland where they were interned in forced labour camps. Villages gradually developed around these camps, partially to administer the needs of the camps and the security personnel, but mainly to accommodate released prisoners who are forced to remain in that area for life.'

'The male adults were re-distributed to a number of different camps in Siberia, some of which already contained US POWs and other foreign prisoners. These camps are totally isolated and have

no villages around them because foreign prisoners are never released and all security guards are accommodated within the camps.'

'The children were kept in Sovetskaya Gavan in an isolated orphanage until the end of October 1983 and then the ethnic Caucasian children were transferred to various orphanages in Vladivostok, whilst the ethnic Asian children went to Omsk and Barnaul, 2,500 miles to the west near Novosibirsk, close to the border with Kazakstan. The selection was based on their ethnic identity to ensure that their physical features matched those of the community in which they were settled. Tracking down the children has proved impossible as they were probably adopted into local families.'

'Most of the male passengers and crew were taken to three top-secret prison camps in the thickly forested 'Taiga' region along the Amur River near the village of Zaporovsk. This village lies 200 miles to the north-east of Khabarovsk which is close to the Chinese border and 450 miles north of Vladivostok. The Amur River forms the border with China at Khabarovsk and for a further 800 miles to the west. All efforts to get near these camps have failed due to the intense security in the area.'

'These three camps are known as Krasnyi, Belyi and Sinii – or red, white and blue. In Krasnyi are all the male passengers who had any electro-chemical expertise, in Belyi are the engineers and in Sinii are the aeronautical and rocket engine specialists. In Krasnyi there was a South Korean research scientist called Chong Yejoon. My informant claims that this South Korean scientist has perfected the design of a remarkable fuel-cell which will revolutionise land transport and many other uses where once fossil fuels predominated.'

'Chong has escaped from Krasnyi Camp with the design of this fuel cell. My informant will be in the concourse of the Baikal-Amur Mainline station in Khabarovsk at mid-day every day for the next thirty days. Today is the fourth of July – a day you Americans

remember well.'

'The Federal'naya Sluzhba Bezopasnosti Rossiyskoy Federatsii or FSB for short, which replaced the KGB, is the same ruthless secret service by another name. The task of capturing Chong Yejoon has been given to a Major Vasily Zhukov. He is one of the most feared men in Russia. He is utterly ruthless and a psychopathic sadistic killer. I expect your CIA has heard of him. To us Russians he is known as 'Ubiîtsa'. You will know him as 'The Assassin'.'

Cavendish glanced at his watch; '19th, we've got just fifteen days to react. Genuine or a 'come on'? You've listened to this already.'

'I don't know, Mark. Apart from needing your technical advice, that's why I asked you to come and discuss this.'

Patrick Merton paused and took a sip of his black coffee and then continued.

'Sadly, over the last twenty years there's been a growing and significant minority of the population in this Country of ours who distrust both the Government and its leadership. Can't say I altogether blame them. Take Nixon, Clinton and Bush; they lied to the people of this Country and if Kennedy hadn't come to an untimely end in Dallas, hindsight tells us that he was only weeks or months away from a scandal that would have ruined him, the Democrats and the reputation of the USA.'

'Every democracy has its lunatic fringe, Peter. It's because we allow freedom of speech that these weirdos are able to voice their conspiracy theories.'

'Granted, but look at the growing support for these nonsensical ideas that 9/11 was a Government conspiracy, Osama Bin Laden was never killed at Abbottabad in Pakistan and NASA never landed on the moon in 1969. Now we are presented with the details of a conspiracy, much of which has been circulating on the internet for the last thirty years, and the carrot to make us believe it is an invention that will make fossil fuels redundant.'

'So what advice do you want from me?'

'In spite of all that it's my view that we should send an agent, but I would value your scientific assessment of this fuel cell break-through.'

'We're all getting there slowly, but if this really is a break-through then we can't afford to pass it up. You have an agent available?'

'Yes.'

'Russian speaker?'

'Yes, but he's just about the only agent available at the moment. Every last one of my guys is out there checking every flight, every 'watch' list, every airfield and anyone remotely suspicious in the run up to the tenth anniversary of 9/11 in less than two months. I'm tempted to make this a joint assignment with BID. The majority of people on that package tour were Brits. There was just one guy from Belgium, a woman from Sweden and our Mrs Hurst. With a bit of luck the Brits will take this on and leave us clear to focus on preventing any Al Qaeda outrage in revenge for the death of Osama bin Laden.'

'I reckon it's worth it. Have you heard of this Assassin?'

'Our guys in Moscow have and judging by the revolting mutilation of Mrs Hurst, this Assassin or one of his killers has just paid us a visit. Right, thanks,' Merton said, getting up from his chair. 'I'll take it to the Director.'

CHAPTER 4

'John Gunn.'

'It's Tricia, you're required back at the 'house' as soon as possible.' 'House' was the soubriquet for Kingsroad House, BID's headquarter building in Cale Street to the north of the King's Road. Tricia Baker was the PA to James Rayner, Head of the Espionage Directorate and Deputy to the Head of BID, Miles Thompson. Prior to his recent promotion, Rayner had been responsible for the Russia and Eastern Europe Department as an Assistant Director.

'How urgent Tricia?'

'Very, what's all that noise?'

'I'm on a yacht in the Solent just off Cowes. It'll take about an hour to get to Portsmouth where I've left my car at the marina. Is that urgent enough Tricia?'

'Probably not, but I'll call you back.'

'OK,' and Gunn rang off. 'Sorry guys, but it looks as though I'm going to have to leave you in the capable hands of Mike.'

The yacht belonged to the Joint Services Sailing Centre at HMS Hornet in Gosport and his crew were men and women from all three Services who were preparing for the RYA/DOT Day Skipper practical exam at the end of the week. As an Ocean Yachtmaster Instructor, Gunn was a much sought-after asset to skipper yachts when he was on leave from BID. He had recently returned from his previous assignment in Tokyo which had ended in a welter of blood and gore in a skyscraper penthouse apartment. He was due some leave so had phoned the Commodore of the JSSC, Colonel 'Jumbo' Edwards. He had volunteered himself for a five day sail-training cruise between Portsmouth and Poole. Helping Gunn was Mike Cooper, a former Warrant Officer who had served with Gunn in the Army and who now spent much of his time messing about in the JSSC yachts. Gunn's cellphone rang.

'Yes Tricia, what's the plan?'

'The Coastguard helicopter from Lee-on-Solent will lift you off the yacht in a few minutes. It's on a training sortie and the practice is just what they want. As soon as you see the helicopter, they want you to release a flare so that they can identify the yacht. They will contact you initially on Channel 16 and then ask you to switch to the local chat Channel 56. You will be dropped in the marina car park. Please come to the Director E's office when you get to the 'house'. Do you have any questions?'

'None Tricia, see you shortly,' and Gunn ended the call. 'OK Zoë,' Gunn turned to a young Flight Sergeant from the RAF, 'you take over as skipper from Ryan; engine on, turn into wind, roll up the heads'l and lower the main. Mike could you grab a flare from that plastic bin just inside the companionway door and light it as soon as you spot the chopper. Tony, you listen out on Channel 16.'

Even as Gunn gave his instructions, the Sea King appeared from the direction of its base at Lee-on-Solent. As soon as the red smoke from the flare trailed from the stern it changed direction and headed for the yacht.

*

'Arthur, get the door would you I'm washing my hair,' Hilda Woodford shouted down to her husband whom she had left seated in front of the TV watching the Manchester

United/Everton match. The Woodfords lived in Salford to the south-west of Manchester in a detached house in East Mile End Road. They had lived there for some fifteen years, socialised very little except for the one high spot in the year when they went on a package holiday abroad. There was an unintelligible response, but the bell stopped ringing so Hilda continued with her monthly hair-dying routine. She towelled her hair dry after washing out the dye and wrapped the towel round her head in a form of turban. There was no noise from downstairs so Hilda assumed that the caller had gone.

'Who was that Arthur?' She asked, putting on her slippers and dressing gown. There was no response, but she could hear the TV. 'He gets deafer every day,' she muttered as she went down the stairs. 'He's left the door open,' she continued to mutter as she shut the front door and turned to enter the living room to remonstrate with husband and find out who it was who had called. She froze, riveted to the floor by overwhelming terror.

A man was standing in the doorway leading into the living room. His head was covered with a black balaclava, only revealing his eyes. In his right hand he held a blood smeared machete. In his left hand, held aloft by a tuft of grey hair, was Arthur's head.

*

The Euro-zone financial crisis and the eleventh hour meeting between the Chancellor of Germany and President of France to find a solution had meant that the staff of all the EU Commissions occupying the Berlaymont Building at the Schuman roundabout on the Rue de la Loi in Brussels had been working late for several days. Peter van den Platt was no exception. A Belgian national and accountant by profession who spoke Flemish, French, English and German fluently, he had just returned from his holiday in Russia with Faraway Travel's package tour to Vladivostok, via several stopovers on the Baikal-Amur Mainline Railway.

Working with the Commission's central financial division, he had returned to find his desk snowed under with files and his computer overwhelmed with e-mails. He seemed to be the last person working on the 12th floor of the European Union's head office. He glanced at his watch - 9.25 - and now full dark. More coffee and stay on for another hour? No, bugger it. It was time to go home. He packed up all the files and placed them in the safe and dialled the closing code. He grabbed his small backpack, went down in the lift and was signed out by the security guard.

He was in luck. As he reached the bus stop on the Rue de la Loi, the 360E bus was in sight. The bus would take him all the way to within 200 yards of his flat in Saint-Lambert in the eastern suburbs of the city. Peter dozed off in the warm bus and it was only because the driver recognised him as a regular passenger that he was woken up at his stop at Place de la Park. He waved his thanks to the driver, got off the bus and walked towards his apartment block on the right side of the road.

There were no cars or pedestrians. The lights in the buildings on either side of the road indicated that most people were either eating or watching TV. Peter removed his keys from his pocket and opened the main communal door to the apartment block which shut and locked automatically behind him. Both lifts would be on the ground floor. He pressed the call button for the nearest lift. The doors opened. Tired and brain working at a snail's pace, he stood aside to let the only occupant leave the lift. Only at the last second did his brain register that the only movement from the man was from his right hand which was holding some form of weapon. It gleamed for a split second in the dull lobby light. Instinctive self-preservation made Peter raise his right hand to ward off the blow.

The back-handed sweep of the razor sharp machete severed his right hand at the wrist and decapitated Peter van den Platt, hurling his severed head across the chequer-board lobby tiling in a spray of arterial blood.

The apartment block door closed behind the man from the lift who went out into the night.

*

After returning from her holiday in Russia, Agnetha Hensen decided that she would sail her yacht over to the island of Ålgön, just a mile and a half from her house at 46, Bastudswägen on Kungsängen, where she and her late husband, Eric, had a small summer cottage. Her adult son and daughter were due to come and stay there, with their children, and she wanted to make sure that it was all ready and fully provisioned.

The thousands of islands surrounding the capital of Sweden form a most attractive 'water-world' of venues for summer cottages and every form of marine activity. The long warm summer months would soon be over and it would be time for the annual crayfish party to bid farewell to the summer with brightly painted moon-motif lanterns and liberal quantities of alcohol accompanied by carols to prepare for the long cold winter.

She packed all the things she wanted to take across to the island into her Saab estate wagon and drove the 400 yards from her house to the small marina where she and her neighbours berthed their yachts. She loaded the contents from the Saab onto a trolley which was chained to the metal railings around the marina. There were always three or four trolleys available and all the boat owners knew the numbers to open the combination locks.

Agnetha pushed the trolley along the floating pontoon to her yacht - a Hallberg-Rassy 35 foot deck saloon sloop. The boats were moored up alongside narrow 'finger' pontoons which jutted out at right-angles to the main floating pontoon. She left the trolley at the set of steps beside the gap in the yacht's safety rail and climbed aboard taking the keys to the companionway door lock out of her pocket.

The lock on the door into the deck saloon had been forced and the door was partly open. 'Oh fuck!' she cursed aloud. Break-ins and vandalism were all too common and all yachts were heavily insured against these crimes. As she bent to inspect the damage that had been caused by something like a crowbar to prise open the door, the yacht gave a lurch to starboard which unbalanced Agnetha and she fell onto the decking of the cockpit.

'Shit! What was that?' she cursed again as she struggled back to her feet and turned towards the stern. Facing her was a large masked man in soaking clothes who had climbed over the stern using the bathing ladder. Her terrified scream was cut short as his machete beheaded her.

CHAPTER 5

Gunn had a clear drive up to London from Portsmouth on the M27 and M3 motorways. He dropped his nine year old Jaguar XKR in the garage at his mews house in Chelsea's Elm Park Lane and a taxi dropped him at the junction of Cale Street and the King's Road. He walked the last 100 yards to the Express Delivery Service office block which housed the British Intelligence Directorate.

He completed the security procedure which was mandatory for everyone going anywhere other than the ground floor. The general public and commercial companies delivered their letters and packages to the ground floor for express distribution worldwide. Large deliveries went directly down ramps to the first level of the basement. Gunn was channelled to the right hand bank of lifts which served floors 6 to 14 and basement levels 2 to 3. The offices of EDS occupied floors 1 to 5 and basement level 1. There were numerous gadgets, gizmos, sensors and CCTV cameras which prevented either inadvertent or malicious access to the British Intelligence Directorate. This security had successfully prevented unauthorised access for some twenty years.

As directed by Tricia, Gunn went to the office of the Director of Espionage, James Rayner, on the 12th floor. Miles Thompson had been the previous Director of Espionage prior to his promotion to Director of BID. Miles and Gunn had joined BID at about the same time and a firm bond of mutual respect and friendship had developed between the two men.

Gunn's specialised area of the world was SE Asia. The Assistant Director responsible for SE Asia was Mike Dimmock and Gunn's Controller was David Morris. Gunn had been brought up in Hong Kong and spoke fluent Mandarin and Cantonese Chinese, in addition to Bahasa Indonesia at a rather less fluent level. More recently he had completed a course in Arabic at the Army Language School in Beaconsfield prior to an assignment in Iraq. He was now in the middle of a basic colloquial Russian course at the same school. A break in the course had allowed him to take a week's leave to instruct on the Day Skipper's Course at HMS Hornet.

As Gunn walked out of the lift on the 12th floor he almost bumped into Angela Purcell, Miles Thompson's PA, who was evidently on her way back from the Classified Registry on the 10th floor with a pile of files.

'John Gunn!' she exclaimed clutching an errant file which had threatened to fall from the pile of files. 'Are you coming to see Miles? I don't remember seeing your name on his programme,' was said in a rush without waiting for Gunn's reply to her original question.

'Hi Angela, good to see you and no, I'm on my way to Director E's office............'

'And he's waiting for you Mr Gunn,' came from Tricia, his PA, who was standing outside the door leading to Director E's office.

'Coming,' Gunn turned back to Angela, 'catch you later for a chat,' and then followed the Director E's PA. Tricia was highly efficient, but erring on the plump side and was slightly older than the other PAs on the 12th Floor. Angela was younger, more attractive and senior to her by definition of her Intelligence Service grade and as the PA to BID's Director.

John Gunn was the physical antithesis of a person who

made a suitable agent. Unremarkable, of medium height and build and unnoticeable made the life of an agent infinitely less difficult to disappear in a crowd or harder to identify by a person who was following that agent. Gunn had none of those attributes; he was 6′ 3″ in height, weighed 196 pounds, had a swarthy complexion and dark brown hair cut short. In his specialist area of southern China he was at least 8″ taller than the average male which meant that he had become used to stooping when it was necessary to conceal his height.

Tricia showed Gunn into her Director's office and then closed the door between his office and her outer office. James Rayner was seated at his conference table with David Simpson, the newly appointed Assistant Director for the Russia and Eastern Europe Department - he had been promoted to that appointment when Rayner had been promoted to Director E - on one side of him and Benjamin Warren, his Controller, on the other. The Director E waved to one of three empty seats at the table.

'Take a seat Gunn.' It sounded very like an order rather than an invitation. Still wearing jeans, T-shirt, cotton anorak and deck shoes, Gunn sat.

'Kak u vas s russkim?' Rayner asked in Russian wanting to know how Gunn's Russian was progressing.

'Ne ploho, no mne nuzhno bol'she praktiki.' Gunn had been expecting this and replied in Russian saying it was 'not bad but he needed more practice' having worked out his answer coming up in the lift.

'You'll get plenty of that. Have you had any dealings with Russians on any of your assignments?' The question was now in English and Gunn could see that Rayner had his personal file on the table in front of him. The file would have every detail of his assignments so Gunn reckoned it was a fucking stupid question to ask.

'Yes sir.'

'What happened to them?'

'Mostly dead, sir.'

'All of them?'

'Yes all of them. The last one was Yuri Volkonoff - ex-KGB - he was killed in the BID safe house in Bangkok. You'll find all of this in that file, sir.'

'How do you know it's in this file? Personal files aren't shown to the agents to whom they refer.'

'I've seen every folio in that file because the Director showed it to me during my last assignment when he wanted me to read what Davidson had written about me. There should be an insert at the front of the file informing anyone reading it that the agent has seen the contents.'

The first Director of BID had been Sir Jeremy Hammond who had retired the previous year to be replaced, not by the obvious choice of Miles Thompson, but by a politically favoured diplomat, Sir Ian Davidson. He had lasted only three months and was murdered only hours before he was due to be sacked.

'What the previous Director of BID wrote about me has been destroyed and I believe that you'll find a destruction certificate to that effect, sir.'

Simpson and Warren were fingering the pencils on the leather-bound blotters in front of them, not wishing to be a part of a dialogue which was hardly enhancing the new Director E's authority or image.

'Yes, that's correct,' Rayner muttered.

'Can you tell me if I'm required for an assignment or is the purpose of calling me back off my leave to discuss the contents of my personal file........sir?' The pause before the 'sir' was not lost on the Director E.

'Have you heard of 'The Assassin?' Rayner asked.

But for the fitted carpet in the office, in the silence that followed the proverbial pin would have sounded like the chimes of St Martin.

'Major Vasily Zhukov,' Gunn broke the silence.

CHAPTER 6

'You've met Zhukov?'

'No sir. If I had, either he or I would probably be dead. When Volkonoff was the KGB's chief interrogator, Zhukov was his protégé. When Volkonoff's psychopathic excesses became even too much for the Lubyanka, he was sacked and Zhukov went with him. It's rumoured that he quickly found employment with the Izmaylovskaya Bratva - the Russian Mafia. Volkonoff was one of a handful of disgraced senior officers from the Soviet era who tried to sell surplus nuclear warheads to Gaddafi and Saddam Hussein before the 2003 Gulf War.'

'You've been to Russia before,' the Director asked in a much less acquisitive tone.

'Yes sir, briefly, on my last assignment. I flew to Vladivostok with Tanya Kazakova on our way to Japan.'

'Of course, she is one of our fluent Russian speakers; right, thank you.'

The light tap on the door was followed by Rayner's PA, Tricia, closely followed by Mike Carrington, the Head of BID's Counter Espionage Directorate.

'Sorry to disturb you sir, but Mr Carrington said it was urgent and relevant to your briefing of Mr Gunn.'

'Yes, that's alright, Tricia. Come in Mike. We'd only just started.' The door closed behind his PA and the Director CE sat in one of the two empty seats at the conference table. Mike Carrington had been the Head of the Metropolitan Police's Anti-Terrorist Command as an Assistant

Commissioner before successfully applying for the appointment with BID.

'Thank you James.' Carrington sat down and produced a small police notebook from his back pocket. Twenty years as a policeman forged habits that were not easily discarded. 'James, after our briefing from the 'Boss' this morning when we were told of the grizzly mutilation of that woman in Indianapolis, I rang round some of my contacts.' Mike Carrington paused, looking at Gunn. 'Does John know the background to this request from the CIA?'

'Not yet and neither do David and Benjamin so it might be better if I give a very brief background and then you carry on with what you have for us. Make sense?'

'Yes, sorry to have butted in.'

'No, that's fine. Very briefly then......' and in less than five minutes Rayner explained the background to the request from the CIA for a joint assignment with BID to find the fugitive Chong Yejoon who had escaped from Camp Krasnyi with the fuel cell blue prints.

'Right Mike, over to you,' Rayner offered as he finished his summary.

'I rang Peter Fahy, the Chief Constable of Greater Manchester, and asked him if there'd been any murders in the last two or three days that included mutilation of the victims. I could hardly finish my request before he interrupted and told me of the brutal killing of Mr and Mrs Woodford. Both of them were beheaded by the killer.'

'I then spoke to Alain Winants, the Director of the Belgian Sûreté de L'Ētat in Brussels, who was amazed to hear that I might know of the equally brutal killing of Mr van den Platt, a civil servant at the EU Commission in Brussels who was beheaded in the lobby of his apartment block.'

'I followed this up, only twenty minutes ago,' Carrington had paused to glance at his watch, 'when I rang Anders

Danielsson, the Director General of the Säkerhetspolisen - the Swedish Security Service - in Stockholm. Mrs Hensen was beheaded while working on her yacht. That only leaves three people from the original eight who went on that package holiday; Baldwin who lives in Chelmsford and the two girls in London.'

'I've spoken to Jim Barker-McCardle, the Chief Constable of Essex, who told me that Baldwin is one of his policemen and he's now in the process of getting him back to the police HQ in Chelmsford. Lastly, I have just come off the phone to DCS Graham McNulty - Head of Serious Crime at the Met - who has sent out two cars with Special Firearms Officers to check on the two girls, Lucy Brahms and Rachel Groves.'

'That's it James, but it looks as though this killer is here and he's only got three more people to murder. We've then got no one to tell us what happened on that package tour. I've also tasked Fiona Ransby to get her guys out on the ground to see if we can save these people and catch this psychopath.'

In the Intelligence Service grade of Assistant Director, Fiona Ransby headed up CE4, the team that dealt with all political, diplomatic and foreign national incidents.

'Thanks Mike. I have to say you've been very quick off the mark. That update leaves all of us in no doubt about the urgency of stopping this killer.'

'No problem; sorry again for the interruption,' and Mike Carrington let himself out of the office. As soon as the door closed, Rayner continued, 'what I didn't cover in my brief...er, John, was the intention of the CIA to send an agent to work with you on this assignment.' Gunn smiled inwardly that the Director E had decided that it was appropriate to use his first name.

'They're sending a Russian Speaker,' Rayner flicked back through two pages of his notebook, 'an agent called Mr

Barnes - Doyle Barnes, I understand from David here that the two of you have worked together before. Mike Carrington's prompt intervention has added a heightened sense of urgency to this assignment so I'll leave you to be briefed by David.'

The Director E stood up indicating that it was the end of the meeting. David Simpson, Benjamin - Ben to all in the 'house' - and Gunn left the Director's office and went down to the 11th floor.

CHAPTER 7

'Victor Golf, India Five, over.'

'India Five.'

'Your location?'

'Alpha twelve, junction nineteen, half-a-mile west of Boreham, over.'

'You are required at Springfield Headquarters asap, over.'

'India Five roger, which one of us?'

'You Marty. Amy will meet you at HQ and will take your place with Sam in the Subaru.'

'Roger, any clue what this is all about?'

'No idea at all, but the message came from the Chief Constable.'

'Roger, on our way,' and Martin Baldwin - Marty to his fellow police drivers of Essex Police Interceptors - turned off the A12 onto the A318 and headed west back into Chelmsford.

PC Amy Rolfe was waiting for the Subaru Imprezza, India Five, as it drove into the Headquarters in Sandiford Road. Waiting with her was Inspector Paul Moor, the Head of the Interceptors. Marty got out of the Subaru and walked over to his Inspector. Amy took his place in the Subaru which drove back onto Sandiford Road to continue its search for drug dealers, car thieves, joy riders and untaxed and uninsured cars.

'What's all this, sir?' Marty asked his Inspector.

'No idea Baldwin, all I can tell you is the Chief

Constable's office is filled with Specialist Firearms Officers and spooks from BID. What've you been up to?'

'Bloody hell - nothing, sir,' Marty replied as his Inspector led him up the stairs to the Chief Constable's office.

'Ah! PC Baldwin, come in,' Chief Constable Barker-McCardle invited, turning away from talking to a group of four men - all in various forms of very casual civilian clothes. 'No need to keep you Inspector Moor.' Baldwin's Inspector took the hint and left the office. 'These two officers are from BID's Counter Espionage Directorate and these two officers are from the Met's Specialist Firearms Unit. Please sit down everyone and I will then quickly brief PC Baldwin who I can see is as puzzled as I was.'

'Baldwin, you've just returned from a package holiday to Russia?'

'Yes sir, I didn't know..........'

'That's alright, in fact it's original and imaginative rather than a package tour to the Costa Brava......er, yes,' he'd remembered that his Assistant Chief Constable, sitting in on the meeting, had just returned with his family from Fuengirola on the Costa del Sol. 'Can you remember the other people who were on that package holiday with you?'

'Yes sir, there were two good-looking girls from London....er, Lucy and ......'

'Rachel,' was supplied by one of the spooks.

'Yea, that's right, Rachel, and then there was an American woman......I particularly remember her because she lived in Indianapolis, which is where I want to go on my next leave to see the Indy 500 Race. Her name was Myra, oh yes, and then there were the Woodfords - they kept themselves to themselves most of the time. And a really nice Swedish lady and......and a guy, I think he was Belgian, worked in some European Union office in Brussels....van de something was his name.'

'Van den Platt,' again supplied by a spook.

'Yea, that's it. Sir,' and Marty addressed his question to the Chief Constable, 'if you know all the names, am I allowed to ask why I'm being asked for them?'

'Yes of course you can. It will become clear in a few minutes. Mr Baines, over to you,' and the Chief Constable turned to one of the spooks.

'Thank you sir. It's Marty I believe?'

'Yea, I'm Marty.......to my mates.'

'I'm Tony Baines and I work for a team in BID's Kingsroad House known as CE4. We deal with all matters connected with embassies, diplomatic incidents and crime by foreigners in this country, other than terrorism - another team, or rather a whole bunch of teams, deal with that.' Tony Baines calm and matter of fact explanation reassured Marty.

'Thanks sir. What is it you want to know?'

'Can you remember during the holiday whether any of you were approached by a Russian.........I mean you must have met many Russians, but was there any incident that struck you as odd....particularly as you're a policeman and have been trained to spot the odd and unusual?'

'I don't want to stick my nose into something that doesn't concern me sir, but if you could tell me what this is all about, it might jog my memory about some incident.'

'You're right, Marty. While you were in Russia, a compact disc was passed to Myra Hurst. Recorded on the CD was some highly sensitive information. The only reason I'm not going to tell you what that was, is not because I'm a spook,' Tony Baines smiled and even succeeded in coaxing a smile from the bewildered Marty. 'But because Myra, the Woodfords, Mrs Hensen and Mr van den Platt have all been murdered, either to find out what was on the CD or to prevent any of you on that tour from passing on that information. You, Marty, and the two girls are the only ones left alive and we know that the killer is in this country.'

'What about the girls, is..........?'

'My colleagues and Specialist Firearms Officers are tracing them right now.'

'I've got their mobile numbers and address – they share a flat in Shepherd's Bush. We were going to meet up tonight and go to 'Thirteen' - that's a disco in Gerrard Street. They both work as secretaries at the BBC in Wood Lane.'

'Have you got those mobile numbers?'

'Yes sir,' and Marty removed a notebook from his inside pocket and flipped it open. It wasn't a police notebook which has all the pages numbered. He copied the numbers onto a blank page, tore it off and handed it to Tony Baines. 'The flat they share is 26B Coverdale Road, in Shepherd's Bush.'

Tony Baines took the torn-off page, wrote down the address and then turned to the Chief Constable taking his mobile out of his pocket. 'Will you excuse me sir while I make a call?'

'Of course.'

He returned a couple of minutes later.

'Thank you sir, I've passed that information to the team tracing the girls. Now Marty, was there anything unusual that happened to you or to the other people on the package holiday?'

'We.....that is, the girls an' me......thought it was a bit anti-social that the rest of the group.....that is, the ones who've been murdered, didn't seem to want to mix with us. Sure, they were all older than us....except that Belgian guy. He must've been only about five years or so older than me. On two....no it was three nights, now I think about it, they all went off together without so much as a "you guys OK tonight" or something like that.'

'Do you know where they went Marty?' Tony asked.

'No......no I don't. Hang on, sir. Other bits and pieces are coming back to me now. I have to say, at the time I was more interested in the two girls. Good lookers and good fun they were too. As the tour continued we often bumped into two or three of them chatting.'

'Nothing odd about that, is there?'

'No, but the chat stopped as soon as we joined them and they started talking about the weather or the hotel.'

'That's most helpful. Apart from that you didn't see them meet up with or go off with any Russians?'

'No....only the Russians we all met on the holiday.'

'Thank you Marty, that's been really helpful.'

'Alright to meet up with the girls tonight, sir?'

'I expect so. Give me a call on that number in a couple of hours and I'll have a better idea,' and Tony handed Marty a card which just had his name and a mobile number on it.

CHAPTER 8

'I think you were a bit hard on James,' this was said as the three men sat in the armchairs in David's office. His PA, Tina, placed a tray with three mugs of coffee on the low table between the three men.

'Yes, I expect you're right,' Gunn acknowledged. 'But why go through all the drama of lifting me off a boat in the Solent and then fuss about what was or wasn't written on my 'P' file?'

'I think his nose was a little put out by his meeting first thing this morning with the Director when he was told of this assignment.'

'What upset him?' Gunn asked sipping the scalding hot coffee.

'He wanted to give this assignment to Tanya, but the 'Boss' vetoed that outright and directed that you were to take on this 'Assassin' and find the South Korean scientist and his fuel cell plans.'

'Ah! Yes, that might explain it. He didn't appear to be overjoyed at Director CE's prompt and efficient follow up to their meeting with the Boss. OK, over to you.'

'However, the 'Boss' offered a compromise by agreeing that Tanya should be sent out ahead of Ben and Doyle's controller to arrange the lease of a house in Khabarovsk for the controllers. She will meet you on arrival at Novy Airport in Khabarovsk.'

'Doyle Barnes arrives in London tomorrow. We have no idea of course what this contact at Khabarovsk station will tell you, but I suspect that this scientist, Chong, has gone to ground either in Khabarovsk or in the taiga.'

'What or where is that?' Gunn asked.

'The 'taiga' is a Russian term which refers to the dense coniferous forest which stretches all round the World between the high northern latitudes of 50° to 70°. The largest portion of this forest is in Russia and Canada and that forms some 30% of the World's forest cover. It is in this dense forest through which the Amur River flows that the three remote 'gulags' were constructed to house POWs and foreign prisoners. Now I'm going to play you a recording of the CD which was passed to Myra Hurst.' David pressed the 'play' button on the small CD player.

When the recording ended there was a moment's silence, perhaps out of respect for the man who had apparently died in his efforts to get this information to the CIA. David Simpson then continued with his briefing.

'The taiga region is filled with every form of flora and fauna which has evolved to deal with the extremes of temperature experienced in those northern latitudes - minus forty in the winter to plus twenty-five in the summer. There are at least half-a-dozen species of deer and large and small rodents. The largest predators are the brown bear and the Siberian tiger.'

'The Primrose Hill Film and Television Company in north London is currently filming a documentary about the taiga as part of a wildlife series they're doing with Simon Benchley - the wildlife and survival expert. Their production team will be based in Khabarovsk and, after a little persuasion, the Director - a Richard Mainwaring - has agreed that you and Doyle can use his company as a cover for your arrival in Vladivostok and your reason for travelling to Khabarovsk. I've arranged for you and Doyle to visit the company tomorrow, so that you know the key personalities.

The appointment is at 10.30 with Charlie Graham, the Producer of the documentary.'

Gunn suspected that the persuasion would have been a lump sum of money which any film company would be delighted to have in addition to the agreed fee from whichever TV Channel had contracted to serialise the documentary.

'Will this Graham guy be going to Russia?' Gunn asked.

'Yes, and it's 'she' not 'he'. Other than that the remainder of today is allocated to administration, communications and ciphers and your usual visit to Tony Taylor in the armoury. I understand from Ben here, who will also be based in Khabarovsk, that Doyle Barnes will be staying at your house in Chelsea. Tina has all your travel documents and flight tickets. You are booked on a British Airways flight to Moscow, a connecting Aeroflot flight to Vladivostok on Friday and a connecting flight on Vladivostok-Avia to Khabarovsk. Tina has the full written brief for both of you covering everything you've been told to date. That's it John. Have a successful assignment.'

'Many thanks,' and Gunn left the remains of his coffee which had gone cold and picked up two copies of the brief from Tina; one for himself and the other for Doyle Barnes.

Gunn and Doyle Barnes had first met on a course at Fort Benning in Georgia when they were still serving in their respective armies. Both had left the army at almost the same time; Doyle was recruited into the CIA and Gunn into BID for an assignment in Hong Kong where his fluency in Mandarin Chinese was to prove vital to the success of the mission. They met again during that mission and on its successful conclusion Doyle joined the CIA department that liaised with BID on all joint US/UK intelligence missions.

On several occasions each had saved the life of the other. On the last joint assignment which took them to the Iraqi desert, Doyle had been captured by a nomadic group of deserters from the Iraqi Republican Guard. There were many of these deserters roaming the inhospitable wasteland of the desert west of Baghdad since the crushing defeat of the Iraqi Forces in 2003. They had never been paid by Saddam Hussein and most were starving and homeless. The only thing they did have was an abundance of weapons and ammunition. Even the wildest of the Bedouin tribes were terrified of these marauding deserters. Doyle had been so severely beaten on both the soles of his feet and back that the surgeons who treated him gave very long odds on his recovery. But he had recovered. Gunn had twice flown to Washington to visit him in the year that it had taken for him to achieve that recovery.

CHAPTER 9

'Yes sir, can you tell me which casting agency you're with please?' The reception area of the BBC's White City building was full of people of all ages, shapes, sizes, ethnic features and others dressed in grotesque soccer mascot costumes. The women behind the long reception counter were sorting out who should go where for the filming of the BBC sports trailer advertising the start of the Premier League football season in only a month's time. As soon as the 'supporting artistes' - extras - had been identified and booked in they were sent to the cafeteria beyond the reception area to wait for the call time.

'No, I am not with casting agent, I am visiting friends. They work in this building,' was said in a thick Slavic accent.

'These friends of yours, they're expecting you?' the receptionist asked. Strange people and stranger incidents were the norm in this building and there was little that bothered the receptionists. Every day they faced anything from Star Wars storm troopers who needed help to remove their fibreglass armour so that they could use the toilets to the macabre figures of Dracula and Frankenstein, as a matter of course.

'No, it is to be surprise, Emma Stephens.' The man had read the label pinned to Emma's blouse above her left breast.

'What are the names of your friends, sir?

'Lucy Brahms and Rachel Groves.'

'Do they both work in the same department?'

'Yes....I think so.'

'And what's your name?' There was a pause.

'Mr Bourne.' Emma was aware of the large billboard behind her advertising the Jason Bourne trilogy of films.

'Right Mr Bourne, could you go and wait in the cafeteria while I find out if your friends are in this building today. Here's a voucher which you can use to buy refreshments.'

'Refreshments?'

'Something to eat and drink.'

'Ah! that is good.'

*

'Sasha.'

'It's Tony. Where are you?'

'I'm stuck in traffic on my way to Coverdale Road.'

'The two girls won't be there. They're both in the BBC's White City building in Wood Lane.'

'How do you know?'

'I'm at the HQ of the Chelmsford Police. Martin Baldwin's a copper - drives those suped-up police cars. He obviously made friends with the girls and is planning to meet them at a disco in the West End this evening. I've just phoned reception at the BBC to find if the girls are in the building. I was told that there's a man there who has been asking about the girls.'

'Got all that. The SFO guys are already at the Coverdale address so I'll redirect them to the BBC and meet them there.' Sasha Lilley, the operative from BID's Counter Intelligence CE4 team, disconnected from the hands-free cellphone, lowered the driver's window and placed the blue light on its magnetic base on the roof. With the light flashing, she then weaved her Mini Cooper 'S' north through the traffic in Holland Road, round the Holland Park/Thames Water roundabout to Shepherds Bush Common, ignoring a handful of red lights and then turned north into Wood Lane. As she passed the BBC TV Centre opposite the Underground Station in Wood Lane, she reached up and removed the flashing light and checked that her Glock 26 automatic was in her handbag.

*

'Blashford.'

'Mark its Chris, security problem; just had a call from Emma at Reception. She's got a guy who sounds - she says - like a Russian asking after two of our girls in the programming department.' Chris Markham was the BBC's Head of Real Estate and Emma's boss and Mark Blashford was the Deputy Director General of the BBC.

'I've been trying to get you Chris. I've had a call from the office of the Chief Constable of Essex telling us that this man is a psychopathic killer and we mustn't let him out of our sight. Armed police and spooks are on their way here now. Is the man still at reception?'

'Wait a sec,' and Chris tucked his cellphone under his chin as he picked up the landline phone. 'Emma.'

'Yes sir.'

'Where is he?'

'I can see him. He's sitting in the cafeteria.'

'Listen. The police say he's highly dangerous. They're on their way and I'm coming down to reception now.'

'What do I do if he decides to leave or go somewhere in this building?'

'Try to keep an eye on him, but don't in any way obstruct him. Got that?'

'Yes sir.'

'Did you hear all that, Mark?'

'Yes, on my way. I'll come into Reception from the back avoiding the cafeteria.'

'See you there,' and Chris Markham left his office, avoided the lift and took the stairs two at a time down to the ground floor.

When it was built in 1990, the BBC's White City building was state of the art office architecture and heralded the 'open plan' concept of that era. The five storey building had a central rectangular atrium with a wide corridor all round it on each level and was reached from the ground floor either by stairs or lifts.

*

The two unmarked BMWs of the Specialist Firearms Officers from the Met's CO19 Command drove into the car park some fifty yards from the main entrance to the White City building. There were two men in each car and all of them were wearing Nomex overalls, kevlar body armour, anti-stab vests and ceramic helmets. They were armed with Heckler and Koch MP5 machine pistols, Tasers, grenades and Glock 17 automatics. The BBC building was almost completely clad in glass so the overt arrival of the armed police would be instantly spotted. The car park was out of sight from the ground floor of the building. Sasha Lilley was already in the car park when the police arrived.

'Can you guys wait here while I go and recce the situation. If we all walk up that paved path to the entrance this man will spot you guys and could well grab a hostage. I'll find out where he is and give you guys a call. Cool?'

'Yea, that's cool Sasha. Do you know if there are any rear entrances or exits to this building?'

'No, but it would be a good idea for one of you to recce that. Right I'm off,' and Sasha turned and walked quickly towards the main entrance. She was dressed in jeans, T-shirt and trainers and had her handbag strap slung over her shoulder with the open bag itself close to her right side. The scene at reception gave no indication that anything was amiss. Sasha walked up to the counter where she was met by one of the five receptionists.

'Yes, can I help you?'

Sasha placed her BID card on the counter. 'Is either Mr Markham or Mr Blashford here?'

Chris Markham heard his name and came over to where Sasha was standing at the counter.

'Police?' he asked in a lowered voice.

'Armed police are here but out of sight. I'm from BID and also armed. Where's this man?'

'He's in the cafeteria.'

'Can I see him from here?' Sasha asked.

'Yes, he's the large man with the shaved head on his own.........'

'Got him. What about the two girls? Are they in this building and do they know that someone's here asking for them?'

'No, they don't know any of this.'

'Where are they?'

'First floor. Radio 2 programming.'

'Can one of your receptionists take me up to them?'

'Yes, Emma here will do that.'

'Do you have two-way radios?

'Yes, they're all there being charged,' and Markham pointed at a row of small radios slotted into a charger.

'Let me have one please,' Sasha took the radio and glanced at the buttons on the top of it. 'Which frequency are you using?'

'Three,' was supplied by Emma.

Sasha turned the small dial to 3 and switched on the radio. 'Right, I'll keep in contact with you. Let me know immediately if he moves. Right, Emma let's find these girls.'

The two of them went out through a door at the back of the reception area and up the flight of stairs facing them. They had barely reached the first floor when Sasha's radio blurted a warning.

'He's just spoken to two of our girls in the cafeteria who must have told him where Brahms and Groves work. He's leaving the cafeteria and heading for the stairs and lifts. I'll try and keep an eye on him.'

Sasha pressed the speed dial on her cellphone.

'Go! you guys - as fast as possible! Come through the main entrance. Reception will tell you where he is. Large man in dark clothing with shaved head.'

'Roger, on our way.'

CHAPTER 10

As soon as they reached the first floor Emma turned right and led Sasha along the near side of the central atrium to a department at the far end of the floor which to Sasha seemed like a great jumble of desks with computer VDUs everywhere. Emma weaved her way through the maze of desks to the windows at the far end where two girls were chatting and drinking from paper cups.

'This is Lucy Brahms and this is Rachel Groves.' The two girls stopped chatting and looked up in surprise.

'What's this.........'

'Hi, my name's Sasha and I'm with the police.' There was no time to explain about the CE4 Team of BID. 'This is connected with your holiday in Russia. There's a very dangerous..........' but Sasha got no further as shouts and a shot sounded from the area of the stairs which did far more to convince the girls of the danger than any explanation. 'Quick, is there a loo on this floor?'

'Yes.....it's over there,' and a frightened Lucy pointed to the right.

'Right, both of you follow me.......now!' Sasha said adding urgency to her order. The two girls followed her to the ladies' toilets. 'OK, you both stay here until I come and get you. Don't open the door until I come for you. Got that?'

'Yes,' was said by both nervously. Sasha made sure that they had both locked themselves into cubicles and then returned to the programming department. Her reappearance went unnoticed in the chaos that had engulfed the department. Some were hiding under desks and others were cowering behind pillars. The man from the cafeteria had grabbed one of the girls as a hostage. He was armed with an automatic and had his back to the glass balustrade encircling the atrium, holding the girl in front of him with an arm-lock round her neck and the automatic muzzle pressed against the side of her head. Facing him were three of the Firearms Officers. Sasha's cellphone buzzed.

'This is Tom, the SFO you asked to recce the back entrance.'

'Right, where are you?'

'Down on the ground floor. I can hear all the shouting from the first floor. What's happening?'

'The target has grabbed a hostage and is armed with an automatic. He's got his back to the glass balustrade that surrounds the atrium. If you go to the far side towards the cafeteria you should be able to see him.'

'Roger.....wait. Is that him right at the corner?'

'Has to be, as there's no one else by the balustrade.'

'Where are the SFOs?'

'Facing the gunman, but can do nothing as he has the muzzle of the automatic pressed against the girl's head. Have you got a clear sight line?'

'Yes.'

'If I distract him so that he takes the muzzle away from her head can you guarantee a kill shot.'

'Yes.'

'Right, here goes,' and Sasha removed the Glock automatic from her bag and moved into sight of the gunman and shouted, 'drop the gun!' at the top of her voice.

It would have been impossible not to react to a threat from a completely different direction. The gunman's head swung to the left followed by his right hand holding the automatic. The instant the muzzle left the girl's neck the SFO fired. The up-angle of the trajectory of the 9 mm bullet from the ground floor to the first floor removed most of the gunman's head in a spray of blood and brain matter. The girl he'd been holding fell to the floor. As if in slow motion, the gunman turned and collapsed onto the balustrade, toppled over it and fell to the ground floor below. Sasha dialled her boss's number in CE4.

'Ransby.'

'Sasha. I'm at the BBC building. The man who was looking for the girls is dead. He was shot by a police firearms officer. I expect Tony has confirmed that the only remaining guy from that package tour is OK. He's a copper with the Essex police. We've searched the body. There was a key card in his wallet for the Ibis Hotel at Heathrow. I'm going to check his room.'

'Got all that. Any injuries?'

'None.'

'A good result. See me when you return.'

CHAPTER 11

'Our usual competition?' Tony Taylor, BID's armourer suggested. He had just finished checking Gunn's two Glocks - the 19 round Glock 17 model and the smaller 12 round Glock 26 Model. He had changed both barrels and test fired each of the automatics. The 'usual competition' was the highest score from 10 rounds fired at a military Figure 12 target from the Glock 17. Greatly to his frustration, Tony Taylor had never succeeded in beating Gunn.

'Yes, OK Tony.........oops, that's my mobile. Just a sec,' and Gunn picked up the call. 'Gunn.'

'John, it's Ben. The Met Firearms Officers and one of our BID CE4 agents, who went to check on the two girls, have killed the guy we think was sent to murder the genuine package tour people. This has all just happened at the BBC White City building in Wood Lane where the girls worked. He was armed with an automatic and took a hostage as soon as he spotted the SFOs. Perhaps it's a pity they didn't capture him alive. They've taken the body to the police station on the Edgware Road in Shepherds Bush for a PM. Can you meet me in basement level one in a couple of minutes? I've got a car waiting there to take us to the police station.'

'On my way Ben,' and Gunn cancelled the call. 'Sorry Tony, our competition will have to wait.'

'Damn! I reckon I would beat you this time.'

'Dream on Tony! Thanks again for all your expertise.' Gunn returned the Glock 17 to his shoulder holster and left the Glock 26 with the armourer to return it to his house in Chelsea. He called the lift and left it at Level 1 into the cavernous transport hub which served both EDS and BID. Ben was waiting by a silver coloured Ford Mondeo.

The naked cadaver of the Russian gunman was laid out on the metal slab in the pathology facility of the Shepherd's Bush police station. What had been the gunman's face was now just a bloody pulp of shattered bone and brain tissue. Detective Chief Superintendent McNulty was already there talking to the pathologist. As Ben Warren and Gunn entered the laboratory, the DCS paused and turned towards them, unable to hide the look of irritation that two people in civilian clothes had interrupted the post mortem autopsy.

'Yes, gentlemen, can I help you?' was said in a tone that really meant, 'what the fuck are you doing here?'

'Ben Warren, Chief Superintendent,' Ben introduced himself, unperturbed by the cold reception. 'And this is John Gunn. Both of us are from the Espionage Directorate of BID.'

'Yes I see,' was said in a marginally less acerbic tone. 'And how can we be of assistance?'

'Have you been able to identify the gunman, sir?' Gunn asked, adding the 'sir' in the hope that it would lead to a little less hostility. It did.

'Yes Mr Gunn,' there was a pause, 'weren't you the BID agent involved in that business to do with the Japanese Mafia last year?'

'Yes; a young officer of yours was killed and a WPC wounded in Victoria.'

'That's the one. Thought I recognised you. You came over to the 'Yard' for a meeting with Commander Stancombe. Yes, he appears to be an Anatoli Vadin from the contents of his wallet. It's a pity we are unable to question him. It was difficult decision for my firearms officers to make.'

'We believe that he was sent to kill the rest of the people

who went on that package tour in Russia,' Gunn continued. 'If he is the same man who tortured and decapitated a middle-aged woman in America, beheaded another woman in Sweden and a man in Brussels and a couple in Manchester, then it is highly unlikely that he would have hesitated in killing the girls in the BBC building and any of your officers who tried to stop him. If he's working for this evil bastard known as the 'Assassin' by most of the Western World's intelligence agencies, then you would have found out nothing from questioning him. He......' but Gunn's cellphone rang. 'Excuse me,' and he left the laboratory and took the call. 'Yes David.' The call was from David Simpson, the AD for Russia.

'The agent from CE4 has just phoned in from the Ibis Hotel at Heathrow. She's in this man's room. There's just an overnight bag which is filled with spare passports, credit cards to match, a cellphone, 9 mm ammunition, but no machete. The machete has always been the Assassin's trademark of execution. It seems he could be one of at least six people. One passport was separated from the others in the name of Anatoli Vadin, but none of the passports have immigration stamps for entry into the USA, Sweden or Belgium to coincide with the dates that those people were beheaded. In the 'text message received' memory of the cellphone were only the details of the British tourists on that package tour, but not the Woodfords - only the two girls and the young man. The passport which he has been using in the name of Vadin shows entry into the UK after the Woodfords were murdered. That begs the question of the identity of the person who carried out those murders.'

'Thanks, I'm at the police station lab with the cadaver. I'll let you know if there's anything of significance from the pathologist,' and he rang off and returned to the laboratory. 'His room at Heathrow's Ibis Hotel has been searched and six other passports and matching credit cards were found. I've never met this Assassin, but I have met his ex-KGB mentor - a character by the name of Volkonoff - who had a squad of 'Executioners' or 'palachi' - in Russian.'

'These were men - and women - who had been brainwashed into killing automatons. They had no backgrounds and were absolute experts at whatever vile task they were given. The CIA experimented with this about ten years ago in a clandestine 'black ops' programme. They identified a dozen or more young men from the SEALS and Marines who had little or no family and then put them through a similar programme.'

'Only half of the men survived it and these were used as professional assassins to kill troublesome heads of state, Mafia bosses in the USA and even extreme left-wing union leaders. When this was discovered after a US election, the new administration disbanded it, but not before an enterprising fiction author got to hear of it and produced some very exciting books.'

'The Bourne series,' the DCS offered.

'Exactly,' Gunn confirmed.

CHAPTER 12

'Hi buddy, great to see you! Thanks for meeting me.' The two men hugged and then headed for the lifts to the multi-storey car park at Heathrow's Terminal 3. 'So John, what've you been doing since I last saw you in Washington.....and when did you buy this great Jag?' Doyle asked as they drove out of the airport car park in Gunn's midnight blue Jaguar XKR onto the M4 motorway into London.

'Jag first.....I sold the TR6 after it was badly damaged a couple of years ago just before we met up in Havana.'

'Hey! That was a close call getting your Royal Navy Destroyer out of the harbour.'

'Too close for comfort.....and I bought this on the conclusion of that op.'

'This the XKR?'

'It is....4.2 litres, V8 supercharged.'

'Real nice piece of machinery.....and what else have you been doing?'

'Not a lot........language and unarmed combat training and a bit of sailing. What about you?'

'Getting fit......hey, those guys in your Field Hospital in Iraq did a fantastic job. That's what the surgeons said at the Naval Medical Centre at Bethesda. Hadn't been for them I'd either be six feet down or, at best, being pushed around in a wheelchair.'

'Good to see you looking so well, but do you really feel fit enough to take on this bunch of sadistic dinosaurs from the Soviet era?'

'Fit as I'll ever be.'

'That's good news. We fly tomorrow evening from Heathrow. We have a stop in Moscow before the leg to Vladivostok and then on to Khabarovsk. My controller is Ben Warren who will be based in Khabarovsk. He's coming round this evening to talk to us about these 'gulags'. Who's your controller?'

'Peter Samarin....his family are Russian Jews who emigrated to the US at the start of the twentieth century before the Revolution. He's been with the CIA/BID joint intelligence department for about five years now. He'll be joining your guy.....Ben, in Khabarovsk.' There was a pause in the conversation and then it was broken as both started to speak.

'I can't.....' Doyle started.

'You don't.......' Gunn said at the same time....a pause and then he continued. 'I really did appreciate that letter you wrote at the time of Claudy's death last year. The assignment that followed gave me time to rid myself of the inevitable anger and self-recrimination. Very silly to get involved in our line of work.'

'A great kid.'

'That she certainly was,' Gunn added as he crossed into the now defunct 'bus lane' on the M4.

The traffic on the section of the M4 between the airport and London was no worse or better than usual, but it was after six in the evening before Gunn reached his mews house in Elm Park Lane. Gunn had just poured a couple of scotches for Doyle and himself when Ben arrived. Gunn introduced him to Doyle.

'Scotch Ben?' Gunn offered.

'Thanks........just a touch of water please.' Ben took the seat that was offered by Gunn and opened a slim briefcase. 'So that I don't start teaching my grandmother to suck eggs, how much do you know about the Soviet gulags?'

'Not a lot Ben, except they were forced labour camps and it was Solzhenitsyn who lifted the lid on them with his book,' Gunn offered.

'That's about it for me too,' Doyle added.

'Right, I now know where to start. 'Gulag' is an acronym of Glavnoe Upravleine Ispravitel'no Lagerya Truda i Kolonii or 'Main Administration of Corrective Labour Camps and Colonies'. The first gulags were built in 1917 at the time of the Revolution. Men women and children were sent to these prison camps for the crimes of 'thinking differently' from the Communist Regime, reading forbidden political, religious or philosophical books, flying the wrong flag, attending church or even being late for work.'

'Perhaps it's worth putting this in some form of perspective on the scale of crimes against humanity. During the Second World War, the Nazis murdered six million Jews and another six million others in their concentration camps. The Communists constructed 1,976 gulags in the Soviet Union stretching from Wrangel Island in the Arctic Circle in the north-east to the White Sea in the north-west and in the south from Vladivostok in the east to Tibilisi in the west. Of these, 112 were concentration camps for women and children, 41 were extermination camps and 85 were psychiatric prisons. From 1917 until Stalin's death in 1953, 62 million people were murdered in these prisons. That's the figure for the current entire population of the UK.'

'Nearly every single major engineering project in the Soviet Union was built by forced slave labour. This includes all the railways that cross the vast expanse of Russia, all the roads, bridges and mines and the Baikonur Cosmodrome - the Russian Space Centre - 120 miles to the east of the waterless Aral Sea. So any tourist who takes a ride on the Trans-Siberian, Baikal-Amur Mainline or any other railway across Russia would do well to reflect on the thousands of wretched, starving, emaciated and diseased convicts who died building them.'

'After Stalin's death in 1953, many of the gulags were abandoned, but we believe that there are at least 400 still in use of which three are alleged to imprison the scientists and engineers from KAL Flight 007 - or so the message on the CD claims.'

'You sound sceptical about the authenticity of that message,' Gunn interrupted.

'I am. The brutality perpetrated by the guards in these camps beggars belief. If any convict escaped or even attempted to escape, the minimum punishment was a beating so severe that few survived it, but if they did then it was a year in solitary confinement in a cell measuring ten by eight feet. No one survived that and emerged sane. If a convict did escape then the guards deemed responsible were given the same punishment. No one escaped. And even if they did, where the hell could they go? The camps were purposely sited hundreds and hundreds of miles from anywhere.

'What about that book......?

'The Long Walk,' Ben helped Doyle.

'Yea, wasn't that about a group of Polish POWs who escaped from a camp in Siberia and trekked 4,000 miles across the Gobi Desert to Tibet?'

'Correct, but sadly a work of fiction....a fascinating account, but fiction.'

'How's that?'

'The author was a Polish Lieutenant, Sawomin Rawicz, who, along with a number of other Polish POWs was released by the Communists in 1942 and transported back to Poland.'

'I enjoyed the book,' Doyle added sipping his whiskey.

'It was a best seller,' Ben added. 'OK, so what's a gulag look like? Both of you must have seen that film 'The Great Escape' - probably more than once as it's dished up in this country every Christmas. That's largely because of the iconic performance of the 'King of Cool', Steve McQueen. Well, the gulags look exactly like the Nazi POW camps. They're entirely built out of wood as that is in plentiful supply and, just like the POW camps they have raised guard towers around the perimeter. They are located in the most isolated places so even if a prisoner manages to escape, the chance of survival is virtually non-existent. That is particularly relevant to your task. If this Korean scientist has escaped, where has he gone and how is he surviving? Hopefully, you might learn something from this contact who will meet you at Khabarovsk station.'

'Do you believe there is another motive for getting us to go to Russia?' Gunn asked.

'In a word; yes. If this scientist has escaped....and we have to assume that this escape occurred around 4th July.....it's now 21st. Where has he been for 17 days? How has he survived? Who was the person who recorded the message on the CD? We have no answers to these questions, hence, John, you rightly comment on my scepticism. I believe this assignment is highly suspect. Please be even more suspicious than me if all of us hope to survive. Don't under-estimate this Assassin. I promise you I am not being over dramatic. John's using his 'Mark Knight' alias; what's yours Doyle?'

'Patrick O'Rourke.'

Ben Warren declined another whiskey and left the two men to ponder the mind-numbing facts and statistics of the cruelty the Soviet Union had perpetrated on its own people.

CHAPTER 13

'Wow! That was a good workout.' Both men had sprinted the last 200 yards to Gunn's house at the end of a five mile run that had taken them down to the Embankment, left up Sloane Street to Knightsbridge and then back to Elm Park Lane via the Brompton Road.

'You are fit,' Gunn gasped, getting his breath back, 'and I could certainly be fitter. 'C'mon, time for some breakfast before we head off for our meeting with this Primrose Film Company.'

After a shower and reasonably frugal breakfast of coffee, fruit juice and croissants, the two men walked to Gloucester Road Tube Station. The morning rush hour was over and there were plenty of vacant seats, but they both chose to stand as it was only a few stops until they would have to change from the Piccadilly to the the Northern Line. They changed at Leicester Square. The carriage only had about a dozen passengers. Tottenham Court Road was the next station. Doyle and Gunn were at the front end of the carriage. When the train stopped, a couple of people got on through the double central sliding doors and four youths got on through the single sliding door at the far end of the carriage. All four were wearing hooded anoraks and scarves wrapped round the bottom part of their faces.

'I think we have a problem,' Gunn muttered with a slight nod towards the other end of the carriage. Doyle turned.

'Seen....will they be armed?'

'Guns unlikely, but knives........yea, certainly.'

The train pulled into Goodge Street and five passengers who had already made their own assessment of the threat left the carriage.

'If they make their move it'll have to be after the doors close. Just before the doors close we'll move towards them so that we're the first guys they have to threaten. Ready?'

'Ready.'

'Now,' and as the doors started to close, the two men moved quickly along the empty aisle in the centre of the carriage towards the far end. As the train left the platform Gunn and Doyle stood between the four youths and the rest of the passengers.

'Think you're so fucking smart whitey........' the sneering retort came from a black youth, the tallest of the gang, who was opposite Doyle. It ended there. Doyle grasped the hand which had emerged from the anorak with a knife, spun the youth round, snapped all four fingers of his right hand holding the knife and slammed the youth, screaming in agony, into one of the metal upright stanchions that ran the length of the carriage and then dumped him like a waste sack on the carriage floor.

The youth in front of Gunn put his hand in his pocket.....and there it stayed as Gunn kicked him hard in the balls. He collapsed to the floor. Neither of the other two youths could do much because they were prevented by the glass panels on either side of the carriage. The train slowed as it came into Warren Street. As soon as it stopped and the doors opened, the youth nearest the open door leapt from the train and fled. The second youth wasn't as lucky. He tried to get out of the carriage but Doyle caught him with a stinging backhand blow which ejected him like a cork from a champagne bottle. Doyle and Gunn picked up the other two and threw them both off the train onto the platform. Gunn and Doyle turned round. Unsurprisingly, the carriage was empty. Perhaps wisely, no one wanted to be involved or required to provide a witness statement. The doors closed and the train continued to Euston.

Gunn and Doyle left the train at Chalk Farm, crossed over the over-ground track on the bridge and turned into a small courtyard of commercial properties off Regent's Road. A small wall-plaque advertised the Primrose Hill Film and Television Company. Gunn pressed the appropriate button.

'Primrose Hill Film and TV,' sounded rather tinnily from a small speaker above the button.

'Mark Knight and Patrick O'Rourke for Charlie Graham.' A mechanical buzz indicated that the lock had been released. The two men went into a small hallway and then up some stairs to the first floor where a pretty girl in jeans, blouse and trainers was waiting for them.

'Charlie?' Gunn queried.

'That's me.'

'I'm Mark Knight and this is Patrick O'Rourke.'

'Come in and let me introduce you to our Director.' The two men were led into a large open-plan room with a number of desks at which sat five or six men and women. Charlie raised her voice: 'hi everyone, this is Mark and Patrick who will be joining us for some of the time in Russia while we film the 'Taiga Wildlife' documentary.' There were smiles and muted greetings and then all returned to studying the VDU screens on their desks. Charlie took them into her Director's office where they met Richard Mainwaring and then into her own office.

'Who provides all the equipment to film this documentary?' Gunn asked having seen no sign of the 'Film and TV' aspect of the Company.

'That all comes with Simon Benchley who's doing this for the Discovery Channel. The projects for his documentaries on the tropical and sub-tropical jungles were scripted and planned by us. This one on the 'Taiga''- Gunn noted that she had pronounced it 'tiger' whereas Ben had pronounced the 'ai' as an 'a' - 'was a fairly obvious follow-on as the flora and fauna are so radically different - except for the poor old Siberian tiger which is almost extinct.'

'Are you going to Khabarovsk?' Doyle asked.

'I am - someone will have to keep an eye on you guys,' Charlie replied with a twinkle in her eye. 'Tell me, have either of you ever been on a set or been involved as 'extras' or anything like that?' Both men shook their heads. 'Here,' and she handed over two small booklets, one to each of them. 'These booklets are produced by a casting agency to educate 'extras' hired in for various aspects of a film, commercial or whatever. It's really good because you do need to understand the jargon that's used on a film set. The glossary in these booklets covers everything from 'honey wagon' - a loo, to 'gaffer' - the chief electrician.

And here's a list I've typed up for both of you with the names of all the people involved from this Company, the Discovery Channel and Simon Benchley's team. Right, I think that's about that, but I'm now going to break the promise I made to myself that I wouldn't ask this.........our Director just said that you were Government civil servants, but I've never seen anything less like civil servants than you two guys.'

'Oh, that's not a problem, Charlie,' Gunn smiled. 'Patrick's CIA and I'm BID.'

CHAPTER 14

'Is the boss in?' Sasha asked as she arrived in the communal workplace and briefing area of BID's Counter Espionage Team 4 on the seventh floor of Kingsroad House.

'She is and wants you to stick your head round the door as soon as you get in,' Zoe Nixon replied looking up from her computer VDU.

Sasha dumped her handbag and coffee - bought at Costa Coffee in Cale Street - on her desk, grabbed a notebook and pencil and headed for Fiona Ransby's office.

'Oh, come in Sasha.......could you just close the door, thanks,' this was added as the door had been left ajar by Sasha. 'No need to look so anxious,' Fiona smiled, 'this isn't your annual assessment, but it is very sensitive.' A relieved Sasha sat in the chair opposite Fiona's desk. 'I know you were here until pretty late last night. Did you find anything?'

'Yes, the man's Russian Yota cellphone which was in his overnight bag; it's a rather poor copy of the Samsung, Nokia, Blackberry and i-phone. Yesterday, after we'd searched his room at the Ibis Heathrow, we discovered that it had the details of the three British tourists – the two girls and the policeman - who went on that package tour in the 'received messages' memory site of the cellphone. I then took the cellphone to Tony who not only speaks Russian, but is far more of a computer geek than me.'

'I'll take your word for that,' Fiona smiled.

'He was able to unearth a pin-protected site on the

phone. That is what took us....him so long last night. In the end it was really simple. It required a four figure pin number and the first one Tony tried unlocked it - 1917, the year of the Revolution. He then produced a translation of the material.'

'You have a copy of this?'

'This is the only copy, ma'am and I'm going to hand over the cellphone to you now. Tony, of course, knows what's on that translation, but he, I and now you are the only people who have seen it. The content is worrying enough, but the implications are far worse.' Fiona glanced at the sheet of A4 which Sasha had handed to her.

'Aaah!' Fiona sighed, 'that at last makes a little more sense of the visit I had from BID's Director just before you arrived and that is why I asked you to close the door behind you.'

*

On Charlie's recommendation, Gunn and Doyle had lunch in the 'Le Cochon Contenté', a French restaurant in Chalcot Road, just a couple of hundred yards from the Film and TV Company. Over lunch the two of them discussed the prospect of searching for the South Korean scientist in the wilderness of the unexplored forests surrounding the gulags.

'What impression did you get when you were briefed for this assignment by the Head of the CIA's NCS?' Gunn asked after they had ordered espresso coffees.

'Patrick Merton? Mainly that there were a whole lot of unanswered questions about the mission and he was pretty cynical too about the fuel cell bit. He told me that he had authorised a whole arsenal of weapons and survival equipment to be sent out to our Consulate General in Vladivostok under cover of the Diplomatic Bag. From there it'll be sent to Khabarovsk. His last words were to treat everything with suspicion. That was my boss, but the bulk of the briefing came from our Russia Department. That's headed up by Gregory Denikin who was very up-beat about the mission. Yours?'

'Odd.'

'In what way odd?'

'The same conflict of views on the op. We have a new Director E........James Rayner. He's been in the appointment for about six months. I've never had a great deal to do with him as he headed up the Russia Department and nearly all my assignments were controlled by the South-East Asia Department. In his briefing yesterday he seemed distracted, but enthusiastic about the op. I have to say it's without doubt the most inept briefing I've had since I joined BID. He didn't want to send me. He wanted to send Tatanya Kazakova. David Simpson......new Head of Russia Department......told me he was over-ruled by the Director at his daily conference yesterday with Directors E and CE and all the Heads of overseas areas.'

'That's not a name I've heard you mention before. New?' Doyle asked sipping his coffee.

'Yes. She's been with BID for about six months. She was with me on my last mission. In fact she probably saved my life on one occasion. Yea....she's very effective and a fluent Russian.....and Japanese speaker. Her family escaped from Russia before the Revolution. Anyway, whereas Rayner appeared to believe all the business about Flight 007 and the escaped South Korean scientist, both David Simpson and Ben Warren....his controller, who you met last night, were highly sceptical about the op.'

'Much the same with me,' Doyle agreed.

'Makes me wonder if there's something they're not telling us.......' but Gunn's cellphone interrupted. 'Hello.'

'Miles, John. When are you leaving?'

'At 19.30 this evening, sir. The flight's at 22.15 from Terminal 5.'

'Just drop in to my office when you get back from lunch.'

'Yes sir,' and Gunn disconnected.

'Your Director?' Doyle queried.

'Yes, wants to see me. C'mon, I'll pay with my card as this is official entertainment.'

There were no more incidents on the Underground on their way back to BID. Gunn left Doyle with Ben Warren and then went up to the eleventh floor where he was met by Angela, the Director's PA.

'Hello John, the Director's expecting you. Go straight in.'

CHAPTER 15

'Come in John. I won't keep you longer than necessary as you'll be busy. Join me over here in a comfortable chair.' Miles Thompson was seated in an armchair with a file in his lap. Gunn sat in the chair opposite his Director. 'How's Doyle?'

'He's fine, sir.'

'He must have been left with some dreadful scaring after that beating.'

'I haven't seen the final healed result, but he jokes that he never was much for sunbathing so keeping his shirt on to hide the scars doesn't bother him.'

'Fully fit for the op?'

'Fitter than me. He left me gasping on our run this morning.'

'Right........' there was a pause while Miles appeared to search for the right words. 'You will know that CE4 found Anatoli Vadin's cellphone.' Gunn nodded. 'But you won't know about the information which was found on a pin-protected site on the cellphone's hard-drive.'

'Other than the details of the package tour people, no sir,' Gunn confirmed.

'The information on that site gave us the strongest evidence to date of a Russian cell operating in the UK and USA which was linked to a number of sleepers, some of whom have been in deep cover for more than twenty years. That information identified the five executed members of the package tour as sleepers, but infuriatingly did not reveal the identity of the double agents in this Country or the USA. The Director of the CIA and I have suspected this for some considerable time - even before I took over as Director of BID - but we couldn't find the proof.'

'When you and I joined BID after the Director, Jeremy Hammond, had cleaned out the Augean Stables of the mole and leak-ridden MI5 and 6, we really believed that we were joining a squeaky clean, efficient and effective intelligence service. Unfortunately, human nature being what it is, it wasn't long before we found out that we had overlooked a few rotten apples in the barrel.'

Whilst he was in no particular hurry, Gunn wondered where this monologue was leading.

'Don't worry, I'll get to the point soon enough!' Miles smiled, detecting Gunn's curiosity...and, perhaps, a little impatience.

'Apart from my immediate predecessor whose appointment was a political aberration, there have been three other 'losses' from BID of which only one.....Mike Soames.....was a double agent actually working against us. We lost Manton and Peters because of mistakes they made, not because of any treasonable activity. Now we have someone or some bodies, both in BID and the CIA who are leaking information either for idealistic motives or for financial gain. So why am I burdening you with this problem?'

'Well, the Head of CIA, Leon Panetta, and I are nearly one hundred percent sure that this is a Russian cell - now confirmed by that information on the cellphone - with tentacles on both sides of the Atlantic. Neither of us is convinced of the veracity of this South Korean Flight 007 message on a CD, nor the story of an escaped South Korean scientist. But we do believe that a joint mission to Russia, closely monitored by both of us might reveal the extent of this penetration of both our intelligence agencies. From what I have said you will realise that James Rayner, David Simpson, Ben Warren and Rayner's PA, Tricia Baker, are currently the focus of our attention.......'

'May I interrupt?'

'Of course.'

'Tanya Kazakova........?'

'........is not under suspicion. I was just about to tell you about Tanya,' Miles continued. 'Tanya is on a very tricky and dangerous mission. Rayner believes that Tanya shares his idealistic views about everything Russian. He wanted to send her as the lead agent on this mission. It is my belief that this was to ensure that no hint of his possible treachery or that of his counterpart in the CIA is revealed. I made a show of reluctantly agreeing to let him send Tanya ahead of you to prepare the ground for your arrival, but I insisted that you were the lead agent on this assignment which upset him. I believe that he's afraid of you and your success record.'

'Tanya has been given a completely different task by me. Her task is to find proof of the treachery in BID and the CIA. She has gone to Khabarovsk to join up with Vasily Zhukov working as a double agent. She told me that Rayner had already made that arrangement. You will bump into her I have no doubt. Please make sure she survives that encounter and returns with you and the evidence we need to finish the task of cleaning the Augean Stables.'

CHAPTER 16

Vladivostok-Avia's Airbus A320 landed at Khabarovsk's Nova Airport at 19.30 hours local time Eastern Russia. The production team from the Primrose Film and TV Company had changed from British Airways to Aeroflot at Moscow and from Aeroflot to Vladivostok-Avia at Vladivostok's Knevichi Airport. Although not voiced aloud, all of the team had had been reassured to see that they were flying on an Airbus A320 and not one of the ancient Tupelov, Antonov or Yakolev aircraft operated by the airline.

On arrival at Terminal 5 Heathrow, both Gunn and Doyle had met up with Charlie Graham. She was with three of the staff that Gunn and Doyle had met earlier that day and four guys from the film crew. Charlie had handed over various carry-on items of baggage belonging to the film crew to both men to add authenticity to their role as members of the Production Team. Once again Charlie had introduced Gunn and Doyle to the film crew under their aliases. After a very slow passage through Russian immigration at Khabarovsk, with its intimidating array of armed police and soldiers, they headed for the baggage retrieval area to collect all the technical equipment.

This caused considerable interest from the customs officials who wanted to see the contents of every single stainless-steel, interior-padded equipment case. Eventually, after two hours, they were all allowed out to the arrivals hall where Gunn spotted Tanya at the barrier amongst the 'meeters and greeters', but apart from brief eye contact neither made any other sign of recognition. They all went out to the car park where two buses from the Parus Hotel were waiting for them. The hotel was a converted 19th Century mansion - an architectural cross between Eastern European Renaissance, Gothic and Byzantine - a couple of hundred yards from the west bank of the mile-wide Amur River.

On the face of it, Gunn and Doyle had a straight-forward task:

'My informant will be at the Baikal-Amur Mainline station in Khabarovsk at mid-day every day for the next thirty days'.

That gave the two agents eleven days in which to make contact with the 'informant', but neither had any knowledge of the city of Khabarovsk. A 'straight-forward task' until Gunn had been briefed at the last minute by the Director of BID that the real purpose of the assignment was far more complicated and hazardous. On the two flights to Khabarovsk, Gunn had toyed with a whole raft of questions which needed answers. The execution of five apparently harmless members of a package tour to Russia required a great deal more investigation. What was the connection between these five people? If indeed, there was one. Was there any truth in the conspiracy theory of the ditched aircraft? Who was this person who had sent the CD with the American tourist? Or had that CD been planted by her executioner? How was Tanya going to balance working with Zhukov - the Assassin - and liaising with Ben and Peter and Doyle and himself? And lastly, was this penetration of the CIA and BID directed by the Russian Federal Security Service, the Mafia or some other agency?

Both intelligence agencies hoped that answers to these questions might identify the source of the leak of highly sensitive information on both sides of the Atlantic, but also an explanation for a series of inexplicable, moderately high profile assassinations amongst the business community of both countries. These suspicions had been confirmed by information discovered on a pin-protected site in Anatoli Vadin's smart-phone. Finding the South Korean fugitive from the gulag was but one part of their mission; identifying the source of the leak and whether a 'black ops cell' had been created in the CIA and BID by the Russians was an even more important part of that mission.

Weary from the tedious process of clearing customs and the twenty mile bus journey from the airport, Gunn and Doyle, along with the rest of the film and TV group, decided that it was bedtime. Shortly after being shown to his room by the bellhop, there was a light tap on Gunn's door. He was greeted by Tanya carrying a small attaché case.

'Good evening, Mr Knight.'

'Come in,' Gunn invited. She closed the door behind her and came into the room.

'I've visited all the members of the Primrose Hill Company, sir, so you are the last person on my list. I have one or two things to give you that I hope will help you with your filming expedition. Now let me see,' and Tanya opened her attaché case which appeared to be filled with maps and brochures and produced a folded tourist map of the city which she placed on the writing desk. At the top of the map was written in felt pen, 'MICROPHONES AND CCTV IN EVERY BEDROOM'.

'That'll be most helpful, thank you. Can I offer you a drink? Gunn said.

'Thank you, no. It's very late. Here is my card.' Tanya held out her business card, but dropped it. She bent down and placed her attaché case next to an identical one under the desk which Gunn had been carrying as hand baggage. She picked up the card and the other case, shook hands with

Gunn and left the room.

The meeting in the hotel had taken place exactly as Gunn had been briefed by BID's Communications and Ciphers Department. Gunn now had an attaché case with a handful of street maps and tourist brochures which had hidden his two Glocks and the ammunition for them from the CCTV cameras.

CHAPTER 17

'Yes Mike, what can I do for you?' James Rayner offered after the call from the Director of Counter Espionage had been put through to him by Tricia.

'May I take a few minutes of your time to clear a couple of questions I have about John Gunn's assignment?' Mike Carrington asked.

'Yes do.......everything quiet on the lower floors then?' The reference to the 'lower floors' was an in-house jibe at the Counter Espionage Department – much larger than the Espionage Department with a country-wide staff of 10,000 including GCHQ in Cheltenham – which occupied the lower floors of the Directorate. Even though the collocation of MI5 and MI6 into Kingsroad House as the Espionage and Counter Espionage Departments had produced considerably better dissemination of intelligence, there was still an element of healthy rivalry. But James Rayner's insinuation that Mike Carrington hadn't got enough to keep him occupied with the current UK terrorist threat level at 'Substantial' was both unnecessary and petty - particularly as the latter had been so sharp and helpful on the current assignment.

Mike Carrington walked along the corridor on the 12th floor to James Rayner's office. The jibe about meddling with Espionage business had been noted, but ignored.

'Yes Mike, how can I help?' was Rayner's greeting as Tricia showed him into her boss's office. Both men sat in the armchairs between the desk and the small conference table. 'Coffee?'

'No thanks. I just wanted to tie off what might be a couple of loose ends from the 'lower floors' which might, possibly because of my fairly recent arrival in BID, have fallen between two stools.'

'Go ahead,' Rayner offered, without any overt enthusiasm.

'Apart from the details of the package tour clients on the text pages of this so-called 'executioner's' cellphone, there was this pin-protected site which indicated that the five murdered people were connected. But the other three..........'

'No Mike, forgive me for interrupting. That's not the case. I promise you that David Simpson and I have been through that information on the cellphone really carefully. I think you'll accept that the two of us have considerable knowledge of Russia, both pre- and post-Federation, and that is not the correct interpretation of the information which your two agents found in the cellphone......'

'Sorry,' a somewhat surprised Carrington interjected. 'Are you saying that Tony Baines' translation of the Russian was incorrect?'

'No don't get me wrong Mike. As I said, David and I have had long experience of both the KGB and the FSB and the convoluted manner in which they code and disguise their information. No, I'm sure your staff translated it correctly......' there was a pause and then an unforgiveable comment; 'but it might have been wiser to hand over the cellphone to my Department.'

'I can't believe you said that! How you have the gall to insinuate that my agents, who correctly dealt very efficiently with a dangerous foreign agent in this Country, were over-stepping their remit is beyond belief. It's quite clear that I'm wasting my time here and probably yours, as you so rudely insinuated when I asked if I might discuss this matter with you.'

Mike Carrington stood up and walked out of the office. Tricia stuck her head round the door.

'Is there a problem.......' she started.

'Oh get out!' Rayner snapped.

Tricia left the office closing the door behind her and for some time sat at her desk twiddling a pencil in her fingers. Then with mind made up she snapped the pencil in two pieces, got up, picked up her handbag and went back into Director E's office.

*

Mike Carrington hesitated as he reached the door to his office and then on an impulse walked past it and went down the stairs to the 11th floor. He headed for David Simpson's office and entered without waiting to be shown in by Tina, his PA. David had just picked up the phone as Mike entered and glanced up in surprise and stood up, politely, holding his hand over the mouthpiece.

'Yes sir, is it a problem with Gunn's assignment?'

'David my apologies for bursting into your office, but I need a simple 'yes' or 'no' to one question.' Even from where Mike was standing he could hear James Rayner's voice on the muffled phone, directing David to say nothing. David kept his hand firmly over the mouthpiece.

'Of course, go ahead, sir.'

'Since the discovery of Anatoli Vadin's cellphone, have you or anyone in your department done an analysis of the information on the pin-protected site discovered by Tony Baines and Sasha Lilley?'

'No.'

'Thank you. My apologies again for barging into your office; you might like to take that call from James Rayner now,' he said in a Parthian shot as he turned and left the

Russia Department office. This time Mike took the lift down to the 7th floor and headed for the offices of CE4.

'Apologies for arriving unannounced, Fiona,' Mike said as he was shown into her office by a member of her team.

'No problem, sir. Time for a coffee?'

'Yes, thank you,' and he took a seat while Fiona leant over to a side table and poured a coffee from a vacuum flask jug. 'Would it be possible to have Tony and Sasha in here?'

'Yes of course,' and Fiona got up and returned with both of them having indicated to the team to hold all calls to her unless really urgent or from the Director of BID.

'I'm trying to make sure that I don't let slip a key piece of information that might provide some clarity to what started as an E assignment, but which quickly developed into a joint E and CE one when Anatoli Vadin arrived in London. Subterfuge, deceit and smoke screens to disguise the 'enemy's' real intent are the norm in our line of business. Now, all of you in this room are aware of the nature of this joint CIA/BID mission to Eastern Russia to find a fugitive from one of the gulags?' It was a question and all three nodded. 'So first of all, Tony; what is your analysis of your interview with Martin Baldwin?'

'I've been thinking about this and the information on the cellphone over the last 24 hours.'

'Good, well let's take your assessment of what Baldwin said,' Mike encouraged.

'From the outset of the package tour it was clear to Martin that all five people who were killed knew each other or had been on previous package tours together - either or both.'

'Right, so if you had a free hand what would you do now?' Mike turned to Fiona. 'I'm sorry, I think I'm treading on your toes here.'

'Not at all, sir. I was wondering what was being done to

follow up on the killings and material in that cellphone and your arrival has saved me coming to you with that question.'

'Ah, good........over to you then Tony.'

'Firstly, a thorough investigation of the Faraway Travel Company; try this for size, sir. What if those five people were Russian sleepers? I'm certain that no one - as yet - has done a really careful check of their identities and backgrounds. So secondly, check out those people. The annual package tour to various parts of Russia is an ideal way of receiving reports and giving instructions.'

'What about the young copper and the two girls?' Fiona asked.

'Here comes a gamble, ma,am. I bet when we check on previous package tours we will find that there were always a few genuine tourists to make the tour look kosher.'

'So why have they been killed?' Mike asked. 'Sasha, any thoughts on this?'

'Two sir; either something has gone badly wrong and these five were punished for that failure, or the people were expendable and the executions were designed to attract both the attention and disgust of the CIA in order to make the Agency believe the message on the CD and send an agent. It's worth remembering that the author of that message wanted the CIA to send an agent to meet the informer at Khabarovsk Station. There was no indication that he wanted BID involved. If that was an aim then it has been achieved.'

'Fiona, most importantly, your assessment?' Mike asked.

'First of all, sir, may I ask what assessment E's Russia Department has offered on the pin-protected site in Vadin's cellphone?'

'You may indeed and the answer is that David hasn't even seen it.' There was a stunned silence from all three members of CE4. 'I've just come from his office. Rayner suggested to me that CE was interfering in an E matter.'

'That colours my response then, sir,' Fiona replied. 'Everything that happened in this Country from the murder of the Woodfords in Manchester to the death of Anatoli Vadin in London is very definitely CE business in support of E. I know that's how the Boss would see it and how we have worked previously when he was the Director E and your predecessor was Director CE. I support everything that Tony and Sasha have contributed and if I have your support, sir, I would task a thorough investigation of Faraway Travel and the backgrounds of the five murdered tourists starting with the Woodfords.'

'Thank you Fiona. You have my full support for that course of action. Thank you all for your ideas and assessments,' and Mike Carrington finished his coffee and left Fiona's office.

CHAPTER 18

It seemed as though he had only slept for a few minutes when Gunn was woken by the soft 'thump' of the bedroom door hitting the glass tooth mug he had positioned for that purpose. Gunn was still fully dressed and removed the Glock 17 from under the pillow, slid off the double bed on the far side away from the door and noiselessly moved round so that he was on the inside of the door as it opened.

'Hi there John, it's Doyle here so don't brain me with that canon,' was whispered from the other side of the door. 'This is your wake up call.'

Gunn only had a backpack and the attaché case which had contained his two Glocks and 9mm ammunition. He had returned the camera equipment given to him at Heathrow to its rightful owner on arrival at the hotel. Gunn picked up the pack and case from the chair by the bed, opened the door and joined Doyle. At the far end of the corridor was a fire escape door unlocked by a 'push-up' metal bar which led out onto a spiral metal staircase down to the hotel's car park. At the foot of the staircase was Tanya.

Nothing was said as Tanya led the two men across the hotel car park and out onto the dual-carriageway to the north-east of the hotel. There was no traffic and the only car visible was a battered Lada MPV. Tanya opened the side sliding door and Gunn and Doyle got in. Backpack and cases went into the back of the Lada. The inside smelt of stale booze, body odour and sweaty feet. It was only when Tanya was in the driver's seat and had started the engine that she spoke.

'Sorry about the stink. This is a hire car and all the hire cars I tried stank. It's not far. I've rented a house to the north-east of the station in Malinkovskaya Street. It's only a short distance from the house that Zhukov uses as his base in Khabarovsk so that Ben and Peter can keep an eye on the comings and goings from that house. Rayner suggested that I rent a property in that street and Miles Thompson agreed to that when he briefed me. I was warned that it would be dangerous, but BID needed proof of Rayner's treachery. It's only 400 yards from the station, so tomorrow - no, today now - we can either walk or drive there to find this man. That OK?'

'Sounds OK to me, Tanya. Are Ben and Peter at the house?'

'Yes, they arrived yesterday and of course made their own way to the house. Peter, I believe, knows this city.'

'Yea, that's right,' Doyle agreed.

'This city is the headquarters of Russia's Eastern Military District.' Tanya stated turning round in her seat which caused the Lada to swerve across the right-hand carriageway. Both men in the back tensed, but the Lada returned to a straight course.

'Yes, I read that,' Gunn replied, 'is that why our hotel was so full of soldiers and Secret Service men pretending to be hotel staff and guests?'

'It's the same in all hotels where tourists and business people go, even in the brothels......so I'm told,' which was followed by a chuckle. 'Now we're about to cross over the railway. To our left is the station. It's that large white building which is floodlit.' It was a very large building and built in the grand style - and to Gunn it seemed more like a palace than a station.

'What does Zhukov think you're doing at the moment?'

Gunn asked.

'He's tasked me to check on all the international flights arriving at Novy Airport to spot the arrival of CIA and BID agents. There were a couple of flights after yours. My task is to warn him of your arrival.'

'How many people are at the house in this street and where is it?' Doyle asked.

'Six, including Zhukov and a nasty piece of work called Georgy Balashov. One of them is a woman. Their house is about 100 yards further along the street from the one I've rented for the controllers....number 57.'

'Is that where you're staying?'

'It is.'

There was silence for a moment as both men realised the extreme danger of the double act in which Tanya was engaged.

Five minutes later the Lada turned into the short driveway of a two storey house which was identical to the houses on either side of it and those on the other side of Malinkovskaya Street. They all got out of the Lada, unloaded the luggage from the back of the vehicle and carried it to the front door. Tanya dug some keys out of her anorak pocket. As she tried to insert the key in the lock, the door swung open.

'Shit!' Tanya let out a muffled expletive and turned to the men behind him. 'Trouble.' Both men were now holding automatics.

Doyle eased past Tanya, followed by Gunn as they started to clear the ground floor, room by room. Nothing had been disturbed on the ground floor. The stairs creaked loudly while Doyle covered Gunn as he climbed up them. Nothing had been disturbed. All four bedrooms were empty. There was no sign of Peter Samarin or Ben Warren. As Gunn and Doyle turned to leave the last of the bedrooms, there was a very audible click which, in the silent house, sounded like the hammer on a blunderbuss striking the flash-pan or worse, the initiator percussion cap of an IED. Both men instantly dropped to the ground, followed more slowly by Tanya.

'I hope that did not frighten you, Tanya. Did you really believe that I did not know of the arrival of the agents from the CIA and BID? Of course, you want to know what has happened to the two agents who have come to look for Mr Chong. Well, no need to wonder any more. Both of them are now my guests and I am sure that they will more than make up for the departure of Chong. I suggest that you go back to London and tell James that the two agents will be well looked after. I have just the place for them.'

Gunn stood up and switched on the light. The small black digital recorder which had switched itself on operated by an integral motion sensor was on the bedside table. Gunn picked it up, switched it off and handed it to Tanya.

'I have to admit to a small amount of confusion. Who do we think recorded that message on the CD in Indianapolis which kicked off this assignment? Was it the Assassin or was it genuinely someone who wanted to warn the CIA about the Assassin? Why were those five people executed? What had they done - or what hadn't they done? Doyle, I think we need to find somewhere where we can do some thinking and that very clearly isn't in this place.'

'Agreed buddy; could be wrong, but it seems that this guy Zhukov has mistaken our controllers for us. Your double act is kaput, Tanya, so where do we go?'

'I've rented an alternative place near the station in Kashirin Street. There was always the possibility that something like this might happen. Rayner was unaware of this.'

'OK.....this place is under surveillance,' Doyle continued. 'That means that Zhukov may know by now that he has the wrong agents. Ideas?'

'Try this, Gunn offered. 'There are six people in that house.....eight including Ben and Peter if they're still there, and if we rush over with guns blazing it's highly likely that either Ben or Peter...or both, may get killed. That sort of action could attract both the police and military and we'll have World War Three on our hands. We need to reduce the opposition's numbers. Let's take all our baggage and get back in the car. I suggest we head off to this alternative place that Tanya has rented. If this house is being watched, which logic says it must be, we will be followed by the guys from number 57. Make sense so far?'

'Makes sense,' both Doyle and Tanya agreed.

'When we leave here we do so stealthily making a show of trying to avoid being seen. With luck we will then be followed. With some skilful driving by Tanya we might be able to jump the guys following us. We then have to persuade them to tell us if Ben and Peter are in that house or if Zhukov has already taken them to this gulag. You up for that Tanya?'

'Can't think of a better plan right now.'

'Doyle?'

'Let's do it. John, you go in the front with Tanya and I'll go in the back on the left side so we have the option to bail out on the same or opposite sides to carjack the guys following us.'

CHAPTER 19

'Right, listen up everyone.......that includes you, Donald,' Fiona Ransby added, noting that he was still typing on his computer keyboard. 'Where's Kofi?' she asked her CE4 team.

'In the loo,' Zoe Nixon offered.

'Donald, please go and get him and tell him this is urgent.'

'Will do.' Donald got up from his desk and bumped into Kofi in the doorway. When they were all seated at their desks, Fiona gave them a summary of the events which had led to Gunn and Doyle being sent to Russia.

'OK, so that's the background,' Fiona continued. 'This is what happens now. Tony, I want you to take the Faraway Travel investigation as that may well involve, not only your ability to speak Russian, but also a trip to Russia.' There were murmurs around the room. 'Quiet please, I'll explain the protocol after allocating tasks. Sasha, I want you to take the background investigation on the five package tour tourists who were murdered, starting with the Woodfords in Manchester. If you need any help you can call on Zoe and Ryan. Tony, you can call on Bryony and Donald. That only leaves you Kofi, but I want you to continue with your investigation into Nigerian financial scams and the deaths of those two bankers.'

'Before you all ask me why we're going outside the UK on these tasks, I'll tell you. CE is operating in support of E on this mission. Director CE has given me 'carte blanche' authority to follow up leads, wherever in Europe, Russia or the USA.' There was an audible intake of breath around the room as the significance of Fiona's briefing sank in. 'Right are there any questions? Tony, you first.'

'If I have to go to Russia do we follow the same protocol as E about weapons?'

'You will contact BID's in-country cell in Moscow which will provide you with whatever you need,' Fiona replied. 'Sasha?'

'No questions.'

'Anyone else?' but there were no more questions. 'Right, let's get to it and let's have this information as soon as possible so we can help our guys in Eastern Russia.

*

As soon as Mike Carrington had left David Simpson's office on the 11th floor, he removed his hand from the phone's mouthpiece and put down the phone. He had no idea what had happened at the meeting between the Director E and Director CE, but he was not prepared to have James Rayner shout at him on a phone call. He got up from his desk and told his PA, Tina Scott, that he was going to see Director E. As he got out of the lift on the 12th floor he met Director E's PA, Tricia returning from the direction of the washroom.

'Hi Tricia, I'm just on my way to see the boss. Is he busy?'

'No, he's not busy,' Tricia replied, and continued on her way without another word.

'Why is everyone in such a foul mood?' David muttered quietly as he followed Tricia towards Director E's office. The door to James Rayner's office was closed.

'Shall I see if he's free?' was said with little enthusiasm.

'Yes please,' David thanked her, still wondering what it was that he had said or done to upset Tricia.

She knocked on the door and listened.......nothing. She then knocked again........nothing.

'Let me try,' David offered.

'Very well, sir,' and Tricia stood aside as David knocked and turned the doorknob. It was locked. He knocked once more, paused to listen and then retreated three paces, walked forward briskly, raised his right leg and drove his foot into the door by the doorknob. The door burst open.

James Rayner was sitting in his chair behind the desk. The seat was turned to the left so that he was facing the door which David had just kicked open. The left side of his head and the majority of its contents were splattered over the wall and Pietro Annigoni's portrait of the Queen to his left. A silenced 9 mm Beretta lay on the carpet where it had fallen out of his right hand. Fortunately, the self-closing mechanism on the door had partially shut it behind David. He turned and went back into Tricia's office.

'Everything alright?' she asked.

'No it's not. May I use your phone?' and without waiting for her assent David picked it up and dialled.

'Thompson.'

'David Simpson, sir. Please come to James Rayner's office. He's shot himself.'

'On my way.'

David had expected even a mild emotional response from Tricia, but she appeared to be made of much sterner stuff.

'Shall I call an ambulance, sir?' she asked calmly.

'Thanks, but no. Please ask the duty nurse from our medical centre in the basement to come here.'

'Very well, sir. Why don't you go and meet the Director while I phone the medical centre?'

'No, that's OK Tricia, I'll wait here for the boss.'

'As you wish, sir,' but David didn't see the furious look

on her face as she turned away.

CHAPTER 20

'What bags have you got Tanya?' Gunn asked as they prepared to evacuate the house on Malinkovskaya Street.

'Just a pack like you. Nothing else.'

'Is there a back door to this house?'

'Yes.'

'And can we get round to the front where the car is if we go out the back door?'

'Yes.'

'OK, Tanya, you lead as you've got the car keys. Doyle and I will follow. Unlock the car and we will put the bags in the back. I'll carry your pack, Tanya. Doyle will get in the back and I'll get in the front with you. OK let's go.' Tanya led the two men out of the back door of the house into a small yard with dustbins and gardening tools and then round the side of the house to the front. When they reached the front they all bent low and climbed into the car as soon as Tanya had unlocked it.

The instant the doors were shut Tanya started the Lada and reversed out of the driveway spinning the wheel clockwise as the MPV reached the road. Then first gear and the Lada shot forward heading west along the street towards the city. Gunn wondered if anyone had seen them or was their charade of leaving the house stealthily a waste of time.

'Got them!' came from Doyle in the back. 'A car has pulled out from the house Tanya told us about. It looks as though there are at least two of them in the car.'

'OK, hold tight guys!'

'Yes, I was afraid of that,' Gunn muttered. 'Remember, Tanya, the plan is to lead them to some place where Doyle and I can jump them.'

'Yes, I know just the place. I recced it yesterday.'

They drove through deserted residential streets, gradually making their way back towards the centre of the city. Tanya was proving to be adept at driving fast, but not too fast. The car following them had neither side nor head lights switched on. They went back over the Baikal-Amur Mainline railway into the business and financial area of the city.

'OK, this is what we do. Very soon I'm going to turn right into a multi-storey car park.'

'OK Tanya, what then?'

'I'll go up to the sixth floor, park and both of you get out. They will follow, but they will have to drive slowly looking for this car.'

'Sounds OK.'

'As they come past us you two come out from both sides, open the car doors and drag out the occupants.'

'I can't think of a better plan so let's do it.'

'It's just possible that it could be a car with locking doors. If that's the case we might need to immobilise the guys in the front,' Doyle suggested.

'Very few cars have locking doors in Russia. Only KGB Zils have that,' Tanya told them.

'OK, but they can manually lock the doors,' Doyle added as he replaced his double action Smith and Wesson .45 calibre automatic in his shoulder holster.

'How far behind me?' Tanya asked.

'150 yards,' from Doyle.

'Coming up to the car park entrance,' Tanya warned them. She changed down, gunned the engine and swung right off the main road into the multi-storey car park. Ahead of them were three lanes entering the car park, all with barrier arms down. She ignored the ticket dispenser and drove straight through the barrier which snapped off like a brittle Italian breadstick.

The three lanes merged into one at the entrance to the spiral access to the six covered floors and the roof-top car park. Tanya ignored all the exits until she reached the 6th floor. It now became clear to Gunn and Doyle why she had chosen the 6th floor. This was reserved for overnight and long-stay parking. Whereas all the other floors had been virtually empty of cars, the 6th floor was two-thirds full and gave Tanya ample options to disguise the Lada amongst other MPVs, of which there were many.

Tanya chose her spot, the Lada screeched to a halt and Gunn and Doyle baled out as the Lada reversed back into a parking slot between another MPV and a van. Doyle went over to the left side of the passage between the parked cars and Gunn went to the right opposite him. Both men could see each other and the point where the following car would appear from the spiral driveway to the 6th floor.

They did not have long to wait. The sound of squealing rubber on tyre-polished concrete preceded the rocket-like arrival of the car which had followed the Lada. It took off as it left the spiral ramp and crashed down on its suspension sending sparks erupting from under the car. Still at high speed it raced round the circuit of parking bays as the occupants searched for the Lada. Gunn had no idea what make the car was, but it looked a lot like a very out of date, four-door Ford Consul of the 1960s era in the UK. It had driven straight past Gunn and Doyle and the Lada on its first pass. They could hear it returning at a much slower pace.

Gunn saw it first from his position. The car was moving really slowly this time. He held out his fist with a thumb-up sign to Doyle and then imitated a gun sign with the two forefingers of his right hand. Doyle nodded. The passenger in the front seat nearest Gunn had his arm out of the window holding what looked like a Soviet AKR sub-machine gun, but could just as easily be an Uzi or Heckler and Koch MP5. Whatever it was it could spray a lot of bullets very quickly.

Gunn moved round to the back of the MPV on his left as the car approached. This time they would definitely see the Lada. The car went slowly past. Gunn moved along the right side of the MPV. He saw Doyle in the same position on the other side. Both of them were now in the pursuit car's blind spot provided that the passenger didn't choose to look behind him.

Doyle held his arm up - their agreed 'ready' signal and then dropped it for the 'go'. Both men reached the car at the same moment. With his right hand, Gunn wrenched the sub-machine gun out of the passenger's grasp and threw it away. With his left he pulled open the door, grabbed the startled man by his long, pony-tailed hair, dragged him out of the car onto the concrete paving and hit him on the back of the neck with the Glock.

The same had happened on the other side of the car. The driver was unarmed and Doyle heaved him bodily out of the car and stunned him with a skull-cracking blow from his automatic. Driverless, the car drove at slow speed into the cars parked on the left side where it stopped and the engine stalled.

Gunn pulled open the back door of the car, only just avoiding a kick from a booted leg which had been aimed at his groin. The back seat passenger received the same treatment as the man in the front seat. Gunn grabbed a handful of hair, dragged the man out of the car and hit him on the back of the neck with his automatic. He collapsed without a word onto the concrete paving and rolled over onto his back.

CHAPTER 21

'How long ago did you speak to him on the phone?' Miles Thompson, the Director of BID, asked.

David Simpson glanced at his watch. 'Between five and ten minutes ago. He'd phoned me in a stinking rage.......I say phoned, but he shouted at me on the phone. I wasn't prepared to accept that behaviour and had come up to confront him about it.'

'What on earth was he shouting about?'

'I was talking to Mike Carrington who had come into my office. He wanted to know if I'd had time to analyse what was on the pin-protected site of Anatoli Vadin's cellphone.'

'And had you?' Miles Thompson asked.

'No, I haven't even seen it, let alone analyse it. James shouted at me not to say anything to Mike.

'But you told Mike that you hadn't analysed the material on the cellphone?'

'Yes, sir.'

'Right.' Miles picked up the phone from James Rayner's desk. As he did so, Tricia came into the room.

'Shall I put that call through for you, sir?'

'No that's alright, Tricia.'

'Very well, sir,' and she went back to her office. Miles paused before dialling.

'Problem, sir?' David asked.

'No.......no...we'll speak in a moment,' and he dialled a number. 'Mike, it's Miles. Would you come along to James's office please.....as quickly as possible. Thank you,' and he replaced the phone.

The two men were standing in the Director E's office. The duty nurse from BID's medical centre in the basement of Kingsroad House had draped a sheet over the body of James Rayner. She turned to BID's Director.

'There's nothing else I can do, sir.'

'No that's fine, Marilyn. Leave the body as is for the time being, but please make arrangements for it to be taken to the pathology laboratory at Maidenhead.'

The nurse left the office to be replaced by Mike Carrington who stopped in his tracks as he saw the sheet covered body behind the desk.

'For God's sake..........' Mike started, but stopped when Miles just raised a finger to his lips.

'I'll be with you in just a moment Mike,' and Miles went out to Tricia's office. 'Not a pleasant business, Tricia. Would you like to take the rest of the day off?'

'Very sad, sir, but no, I'm alright.'

'Good for you.' Miles returned to Rayner's office closing the door as firmly as he could with its broken lock.

'Suicide?' Mike asked quietly raising his eyebrows.

'Seems so. Not a pleasant sight. What was being discussed by you and James, which triggered his tantrum with David?'

'I had asked him if I could drop by his office to discuss certain aspects of Gunn's assignment which concerned CE. Even that simple request by me generated a cynical comment inferring I hadn't got enough to occupy myself with CE matters. I chose to ignore that and came in here.'

'Go on,' Miles encouraged.

'I told him I wanted to talk about the pin-protected site on Vadin's cellphone and the implication that the murdered tourists were all connected.' Mike Carrington paused.

'Yes, and his response?'

'I didn't get any further. James interrupted me and said that I didn't have enough experience to understand the convoluted way in which the Russians couched their espionage language and that the analysis that he and David, here,' Mike glanced at David Simpson, 'had applied to the material gave a totally different explanation.'

'And was that true?' Miles turned to David.

'No sir, there was no analysis. Neither he,' and David nodded his head in the direction of the sheet covered body, 'nor I had even seen it.'

'Mike, you then went to David who confirmed what he's just told us. James had expected you to do that and presumably wanted to tell David to say nothing, but as you were at that stage talking to Mike he shouted at you. Yes?'

'Yes,' both men said in unison.

'Right I'm clear on that now.' At that moment, there was knock on the door and Tricia came into the office.

'May I take you up on your offer, sir, of going home please?' she asked the Director.

'Yes, of course.'

'Thank you sir,' she turned and stopped by the door. 'I'll have to get that repaired tomorrow,' and then she left the office closing the door behind her. Miles gave the slightest nod of his head towards the door and then continued.

'I would like to continue this discussion in my office so that we can let the medics remove the body.' The three men left the office. Tricia watched them go.

'Shit!' she swore aloud, snapping another pencil she'd been holding.

*

'OK guys this is how I plan to do this investigation into the package tour people. Our boss says she wants results quickly so I intend to get all three of us working to speed up results. That may well mean all of us going abroad at some stage. Any suggestions when I've finished are welcome.' Sasha Lilley was briefing her two assistants, Zoe Nixon and Ryan Owen, in one of CE4's three interview rooms.

'I'm going up to Manchester to hunt through the records of some fifteen churches in the Salford District. The Greater Manchester Police have told us that the Woodfords had lived all their lives in the Salford area so that will be tedious but fairly straight forward to prove that information either right or wrong.'

'Ryan, I would like you to check out the Woodfords with the Criminal Record Board......and ask for an enhanced report, not a standard one. Don't hesitate to flash your BID ID. Depending on that result, can you then move on to the National Archives at Kew.'

'Zoe, you can come up north with me, but I want you to go to the General Register Office at Southport in Merseyside where they now hold all the birth, marriage, divorce and death certificates which used to be at Somerset House. Please trawl through those records. You will both need DOBs and place of birth. Photocopy the back page of their passports, here,' and Sasha handed over the passports which had been found by the police who had searched the Woodford's house. 'OK, questions?'

'Any steer on what we're looking for, Sasha?' Ryan asked.

'Sure, the material on the pin-protected site in the cellphone indicated that these five people, however harmless they may seem, are deep cover 'sleepers' waiting to be activated. The Soviet Union has been doing this for years. Don't be fobbed off when you're talking to neighbours who tell you that the Woodfords or any of the others were the nicest people ever.'

'Are the Russians still in the game of establishing

sleepers in western democracies?' Zoe asked.

'On the face of it, yes, but this man Zhukov, who calls himself the Assassin, is Soviet-era KGB and now possibly connected with the Russian Mafia. Don't under-estimate these guys.......' but she was interrupted as the door opened and Fiona put a head round it.

'Sorry to interrupt. Sasha, just a quick word.'

Sasha got up and left the interview room closing the door behind her.

'More developments; Director E has just topped himself. He blew his brains out with a silenced Beretta. Please emphasise, if you haven't already, how dangerous this mission is.'

Without a word, Sasha returned to the interview room and passed on the information to her two colleagues.

*

Tony Baines was in another interview room with Bryony Whistler and Donald Masterson. He had just passed on the news about the Head of E's suicide to his colleagues.

'To start with, I'm going to work on my own on this, guys, but I promise, the moment it looks like hard work I'll call you two in. I intend to start with the London office of Faraway Travel - it's in Gresham Street in the City. There are branches in Manchester and Edinburgh in the UK and overseas branches in Moscow and the major Western capitals. While I'm away could you both trawl the internet to see what you can find out about the company and the people who sign up for these package tours to Russia.'

CHAPTER 22

Gunn stepped back from the two unconscious men on his side of the car. Doyle came round from the other side of the Gaz Volga saloon, dragging the body of the driver. The two men were joined by Tanya. She bent down and looked more closely at the faces of the three men.

'These all come from house number 57.'

'That means there are three left.......plus Ben and Peter. The sooner we get back there the better,' Gunn urged the other two. 'Anyone got cable ties and tape handy?'

'Sure,' and Tanya went back to the Lada and returned with the ties and tape.

'Did the boss tell you of his suspicions about Rayner?' Gunn asked Tanya.

'Yes.....in some detail and he said that the CIA also had a problem,' she answered, glancing at Doyle.

'That's right. Leon Panetta told me that it was not only BID that had a problem, but we also had one,' Doyle offered and then continued, 'in our case it wasn't Denikin, our Head of the Russia Section, it's Merton, our Head of National Clandestine Service and another person as yet unidentified.'

'My boss believes that this whole business of the fugitive South Korean scientist was dreamt up by the Russians because both the CIA and BID were getting too close. It was a smoke screen to distract us,' Gunn explained what he'd been told by his Director.

'Panetta reckoned that the author of that CD wanted the CIA to send an agent. The Russians would then capture the agent and use him as a bargaining chip to save Merton's arse,' Doyle said. 'Do we go through with the meeting at the station?'

'It seems as though this mission is compromised, but I reckon we've got to go through with the RV at the station, however risky, to close the loop on that CD message, if for no other reason,' Gunn replied.

'OK, right, let's load this lot into the Lada.'

'Just how deep do you think this cancer goes that we were warned about before this mission?' Doyle asked as the three of them got on with cable-tying hands and feet and placing masking tape over mouths.

'I've no idea, but certainly they - whoever 'they' are.......Federal Security Service, redundant KGB or Mafia, must know everything about us. No wonder they picked up Ben and Peter so quickly. They were probably waiting for them at the airport and picked them up while you were waiting for us, Tanya. Gunn's cellphone interrupted him. 'It's a text from BID.' Gunn opened the message. 'It gets worse, guys.'

'What's that?'

'Our Director of Espionage, James Rayner, has just blown his brains out in the office.'

'Preferred that to a trial and disgrace?'

'Possibly, so this does appear to be a Russian cancer. Come on. Let's make the most of grabbing this bunch. I suggest we dump them all in the Lada and then head back to Malinkovskaya Street and pay a visit to number 57 where this car came from. Let's hope that Ben and Peter are there.'

Tanya drove the Lada over to the Gaz and they loaded the three bodies unceremoniously into the rear compartment of the MPV with the bags. The AKR sub-machine gun went into the boot of the Gaz along with the Gaz driver's 9 mm Stechkin.

'You lead the way Tanya and we'll follow. Stop well short of 57 and come to the rescue if we call you on your cellphone. Doyle got into the driver's seat and reversed the Gaz away from the boot of the car that had halted it. With Tanya leading in the Lada, the two cars set off in convoy leaving the multi-storey car park by the entrance lane, driving over the smashed barrier.

The streets were still deserted and it only took a little over ten minutes before the Lada, followed by the Gaz, turned into Malinkovskaya Street. The Lada pulled over to the right side and stopped. Doyle took his automatic out of his shoulder holster and pushed it into the waistband of his jeans.

'Ready?' he asked

'Ready, let's go,' Gunn replied. The Gaz drove off without lights and turned across the road into the driveway of the house that Doyle had identified earlier. Although they had found some keys on the man in the passenger seat of the Gaz, they decided to break the lock rather than fiddle around with keys in the dark. Doyle waited by the front door of the house while Gunn went round to the back to foil any attempt to escape. He slammed his foot into the door which burst open. Doyle caught sight of a figure dashing out of a front room of the house towards the back where a door led out into the yard. He stayed just inside the front door covering the hall and the stairs up to the first floor.

There was a high-pitched shriek from the back and a few seconds later Gunn appeared, pushing a woman who was gripped in a suffocating arm-lock around her neck. Doyle switched on the lights and then checked the ground floor rooms while Gunn hung on to his prisoner. No one. He went up the stairs and checked the bedrooms. Plenty of signs of occupation, but no one was there and not a sign of Zhukov, Balashov or Ben and Peter. Doyle came down the stairs and dialled the number for Tanya's cellphone.

'OK Tanya, come and join us. The house is secure. We'll need your cable ties and tape.'

CHAPTER 23

The three men left Director E's office and went along the corridor of the 12th floor to the Director's office. Miles Thompson paused in his PA's office.

'Hold all calls please Angela unless you consider them urgent or it's from the Cabinet Office or the ISC. Go in and help yourselves to coffee or tea,' was directed at Mike Carrington and David Simpson. He then told Angela of James Rayner's suicide and gave her one more instruction before joining the other two in his office. David Simpson was reading a text on his cellphone.

'It gets worse, sir. Ben Warren and Peter Samarin have been abducted by Zhukov. Gunn and Barnes have got hold of the four Russians who abducted them.

'Tanya?' Miles Thompson asked.

'She's OK and now with Gunn and Doyle.

'Thank God for that,' was said by the Director.

'But Zhukov had already gone,' David continued, 'as have Warren and Samarin. That's it.'

'Thank you David. I won't keep you any longer as you will be busy with Gunn's assignment. I'll be taking over as Director E until I appoint a replacement for James Rayner. Please deal directly with me on every aspect of this assignment.'

'Very well, sir,' and David left the Director's office. There was a moment's silence while Miles poured himself a cup of coffee.

'Before we tackle the problem of James's death I must

share my thoughts with you on the penetration of BID by what now seems to be a Russian cell operating in both this Country and the USA. This also affects the CIA and both Leon Panetta and I agreed that this current assignment should go ahead as a joint CIA/BID one as it might well force various people to show their hand. I think that has already happened. There can be little doubt that this is Russian-driven espionage, but whether it is FSB or another agency has yet to be established. Until his death a short while ago, James and Russia Department's David and Ben have all been watched closely by our Head of Security. I would like to think that David and Ben are clean, but I don't have the proof....yet.....hence the assignment to Eastern Russia. A short while ago, John Gunn was sitting in that chair hearing exactly the same information as you. You now know as much as I do, but I'm hoping that your CE4 team and Gunn may be able to identify the moles and double agents. Right, enough of that, now let me turn to the bizarre death of James Rayner.'

'Mike, you have years of police experience, much of that as a detective. While you were in James's office just now did you notice anything odd that might contradict the obvious deduction that James committed suicide?' Miles sipped his coffee giving Mike Carrington time to cast his mind back to the scene in Director E's office.

'I have to admit that I was suffering from mild shock when confronted with James's sheeted body. Initially I had no reason to doubt the suicide theory.'

'Take your time. David told us that the door to the office was locked. He had tried to open it. He then broke the door open by kicking it. I was the next person into the office. Tricia was still by her desk when I went through into James' office. The nurse was the next person who entered the office and left after covering James with a sheet. You were the next person who came into the office.'

'Something to do with the Beretta perhaps? James is right handed and the gun appeared to have fallen where I would expect to find it if he'd shot himself,' Mike muttered uncertainly.

'No, not the gun. Picture in your mind the door with its broken lock.'

'Yes, I can see it now in my mind's eye......what was wrong with the door?......no not the door.' Mike Carrington had his eyes closed as he forced his mind to recreate the scene in the office.

'Go on, I think you're nearly there,' Miles encouraged.

'Not the door.....it was the lock.....the broken lock. If it was locked when David arrived then the key should have been on the inside.......or on the carpet if the impact of David's kick had ejected the key. But it wasn't......I mean in the lock or on the floor.'

'Well done.......so now tell me how that key managed to find its way into the lock on the inside of the door by the time the three of us left the office.'

'Tricia!'

'Exactly....... James Rayner was murdered. I believe that the rather unattractive dumpy lady who has been with James as a PA ever since he joined BID is probably the key person in this cell and probably even outranked James.'

'Shouldn't we be arresting her........at least on suspicion of being involved in James's death?' Mike Carrington said anxiously.

'Not just yet. When you and David came into this office, I gave Angela my authorisation code to order the lockdown of this building. Jack Barclay, our Head of Security, will have sealed this building. No one will be leaving Kingsroad House, unless they choose to jump off the roof.'

*

As soon as the three men had left her office, Tricia opened the safe and removed the 9mm Smith and Wesson automatic which she put in her Louis Vuiton-copy carrier bag after removing her trainers. The trainers replaced her smart high-heeled court shoes. She looked round the office. Nothing else she needed. 'Had those men noticed the key?' she wondered. 'No,' she reassured herself, 'they would have been far more concerned about the suicide of that idiot James who had become such a liability.'

Tricia looked out of her door into the corridor. No one. Carrying the bag with her shoes and automatic, she hurried along the corridor to the lifts and pressed the call button. 'Come on, come on,' she urged the sedate progress of the lift from the 7th to the 12th floor. The lift arrived and the doors opened. Ground floor button was pressed and the lift descended. The 'G' indicator lit and the doors opened. Only twenty yards, past Security, into the enclosed turnstile and then out of the doors and away. She gripped her pass tightly in her hand. It was the last time she would have to swipe it at Security before entering the turnstile. 'Why was Jack Barclay, the Head of Security, talking to the guards at the turnstiles?'

He turned towards her. They knew. The building had been locked down. Her hand plunged into the bag and grasped the automatic. Men seemed to appear from all sides and her arms were firmly pinned against her sides. Jack Barclay walked towards her.

'I'll take that bag, thank you Miss Baker.'

CHAPTER 24

The main UK branch of the travel agent, Faraway Travel at Gresham Street in the City, seemed as good a place as any to start his investigation. Tony Baines and the other operatives in CE4 had been left in no doubt by their boss Fiona Ramsay about the need to complete the investigation as quickly as possible in support of an 'E' assignment in Russia.

There was nothing unusual about the agency when he arrived there mid-morning. So far, the weather in July had been dreadful, but on that morning the sun was shining and it was almost warm enough for Tony to remove his jacket. The plate glass frontage of the travel agent was filled with advertising material for package tours to every part of Russia including cruises on the Volga and Amur Rivers, Black Sea and Caspian Sea.

Inside the agency there was a long bar-like counter on the left with fixed uncomfortable-looking swivel plastic seats. Three girls were dealing with prospective clients. On the right were some less uncomfortable-looking plastic chairs for those waiting to buy a holiday in Russia. There was a ticket dispenser with a sign inviting all customers to take a ticket and await their turn. Tony took ticket number 47. 'Had there really been that number of clients that morning?' he wondered as he picked up a couple of brochures and discovered that the seats on the right were probably just as uncomfortable as those at the counter. Waiting his turn gave Tony a chance to watch all the customers and listen to the 'sales patter' from the Travel Advisors – this was the title given to the girls at the counter beside their name plates. The girl nearest to him -Yvonne, on her name plate - was 'advising' a middle-aged couple. There was no trace of a Russian accent. It was a good solid south London accent. Tony heard Yvonne quote a price for a ten day Volga cruise. The man said that they would think about it and the couple left the agency. Number 45 appeared on the 'Next for Service' screen. A woman in her forties, Tony estimated, got up and went to Yvonne near him.

'My name's Yvonne, what can I do to help you, madam?' was asked cheerily by the girl. But instead of answering the girl's query, Tony saw the woman remove a card from her wallet which she placed in front of Yvonne. The girl glanced at the card. 'Oh, you'll be on the Aral Sea Adventure package from 8th to 18th October.'

The woman had said nothing. 'How the hell did the girl know where she wanted to go? And what was on that card the woman had placed on the counter in front of the girl?' Tony wanted to know. There was a stack of brochures on the counter just to the left of the woman. Tony got up and walked to the counter where he grabbed a brochure and very clumsily upset the stack over the counter in front of the woman.

'Sorry, really clumsy of me. Let me tidy up the brochures.'

'No, don't bother with that, thank you,' the woman replied and even gave Tony a smile. He returned to his seat remembering to take one of the brochures. The plastic card had read - FARAWAY TRAVEL, PRIVILEGE MEMBERSHIP CARD - and under that in bold type was a six or seven figure number. Number 46 came on the screen and a man got up and went to the girl on Yvonne's left. The woman with the privilege membership card finished her business with Yvonne and left the agency. 47 appeared on the screen and

Tony went over to Yvonne.

'Sorry again about the brochures.'

'Not a bit, sir. They shouldn't have been there but we hadn't got round to putting them in the display stands. Now how can I help you?....I don't think we've seen you before, have we?'

'No, it's my first visit. I was thinking of a cruise on the Amur River.'

'This year, sir?'

'Yes, when does it start to get really cold?'

'Well sir, the last cruise is from 22nd to 29th October. From mid-November to the end of March, the Amur River freezes over. In winter it can go as low as minus 25 Centigrade.'

'Wow! That really is cold. Do you have any vacancies for a cruise in August?' Tony asked, keeping half an eye on the man on his right. Exactly the same procedure had happened there. The man had produced a card and was told that he would be on the Trans-Siberian Railway package leaving Moscow on 10th September and reaching Vladivostok via Lake Baikal on 20th September.

'Just a moment, sir; bear with me while I check,' and Yvonne turned to her computer VDU and tapped away on her keyboard. While she was doing that, the agency supervisor - Tony read that from the lapel badge above her left breast – came over to Yvonne.

'Excuse me sir. Yvonne, I want you to take the early lunch today.' The supervisor looked at her watch. 'That will be in ten minutes. OK?' Yvonne looked up from her VDU.

'Very well Mrs Garin, I'll go after I've helped this gentleman.' The lapel badge stated that the supervisor was Katherin Garin, but she evidently did not encourage her staff to address her by her given name. The accent was very Slavic.

'That is good, sorry to interrupt, sir,' and supervisor

Garin returned to her desk at the far end of the agency.

'Is it just you, sir?'

'Yes, just me.'

'There's a vacancy on the cruise from 6th to 13th August. You would fly from London Heathrow on 4th August, changing at Moscow and Vladivostok. The night of 6th is in the Boutique Hotel in Islomina Street – that's very close to the Amur River and then an outside cabin on the Amur Star. How does that sound, sir?'

'Excellent. I need to grab a sandwich or something as I had no breakfast this morning. Can you recommend somewhere close?'

'Yes sir. I'm having my lunch break as soon as you are happy with the cruise. I can show you where I go for lunch.....it's only sandwiches and snacks, but if you wanted a proper.....'

'No...no, sandwiches would be great. Now what do I have to do to secure that cruise?'

'It's only three weeks away sir, so we would need full payment now.'

'Good. Please take it out of that card,' and Tony handed over his Visa credit card courtesy of BID. Yvonne did the necessary with the credit card, handed the machine over to Tony who tapped in his pin and the two of them then left the agency.

Yvonne led Tony to a Prêt à Manger only two hundred yards from the Travel Agent where both picked up a sandwich pack and coffee and sat on high stools with a matching high-legged small circular table between them.

'So how long have you worked for Faraway Travel?' Tony asked as he opened his BLT pack.

'Just over a year now.'

'Your supervisor is Russian?'

'Yes, bit of an ogre, but not too bad really.'

'Does Faraway Travel train you?' Tony tried to keep the questioning as casual as possible, but Yvonne was quite keen to talk about her job.

'Yes, there's a place up in Manchester where all the training is done. We spend a fortnight there before they let us loose at a branch under supervision.'

'When I was so clumsy with those brochures, I saw that the lady had a Faraway Travel membership card. Does that give you discounts and can I apply for one?'

'No, I'm afraid not, si.....'

'My name's Tony. Please don't bother with the 'sir' bit.

'OK Tony, they tell us that those cards are very special and only for people who have frequently travelled with Faraway Travel.'

'So how often must I use Faraway Travel before I might be eligible to apply?' There was silence for a moment.

'No one has ever asked that question before. Tamasin and Vicky.......the other two girls in the office with me today.....we all trained together and were told how the privilege card system worked, but not how or why these people had those cards. It's a very simple system, Tony, all we have to do is enter the numerical code on the card into a slot on the privilege card page of our computers and it produces the package tour and dates automatically.'

'And payment?'

'Again, that's automatically deducted from the person's Faraway Travel account.' Tony reckoned that he had heard enough and any more questioning might cause gossip amongst the 'Advisors' which would reach the ears of the 'ogre' at her supervisor's desk.

'Thanks so much for showing me this place and for the river cruise. Do you get to go to Russia?'

'Oh yes, each of us does one trip a year as a tour courier.'

'Seems like an interesting job. I'll be on my way and

thanks again. Bye,' and Tony got off the stool and left Prêt à Manger heading for St Paul's Underground Station.

A simple interrogation of a girl in a travel agent appeared to have revealed a Russian network of travel agents in Europe and the USA...and possibly elsewhere in the World.....that had a fool-proof way of briefing its agents and gathering intelligence without risking any form of electronic communication which could be hacked or listened into. Brilliant! But was this Russia's State Security Service - the FSB - or something set up by the disbanded KGB....or the Mafia....or....or...and a host of other possibilities went through Tony's mind as he made his way down the steps into the Underground on his way back to BID.

CHAPTER 25

'I'll drop you off at Manchester's Piccadilly Station, Zoe. You can catch a connecting train from there to Merseyside. Once you've finished checking on the births, marriages and deaths.....particularly deaths in infancy.....and any missing records or certificates, please get me on my mobile.' Sasha dropped Zoe off at the station and then continued westward to Salford to start her search into the background of the Woodfords.

Her GPS navigator in the Mini Cooper S took her to the Woodford's house in East Mile End Road. The house stood on its own with about half an acre of garden surrounding it. Beyond that was farm land, but there was one other house a further 100 yards along the road. Sasha drove past the Woodford's house and stopped outside the house beyond it. As she walked up the short path to the front door, she was greeted by a very fat Labrador and a marmalade cat who eyed her suspiciously from a window ledge where it was sunning itself. The door was opened as soon as she rang the bell.

'Oh hello, I'm Sasha Lilley and I work with the police,' holding up her BID ID. 'I'm making a few more enquiries about the murder of Mr and Mrs Woodford. Can you spare a few minutes to help me with those enquiries please?' The door had been opened by a plump woman of indefinable age between forty and sixty who eyed Sasha suspiciously.

'What d'you want to know.' No invitation to come into the house.

'How long had you known Hilda and Arthur?'

'They moved into that 'ouse in '95.....just before Christmas. It were a bad year for snow and my 'enry 'elped them clear snow from path.'

'Did you see much of them?'

'Not really, luv.' The overt hostility had gone, but there still remained the suspicion of authority, particularly police authority. 'Kept themselves to themselves they did. Must've had a bit of money put by 'cos they went on 'oliday every year in July.'

'Did you know where.'

'Where what, luv?'

'Where they went on holiday.'

'Oh aye, it were Russia......who'd want to go there?'

'Did they ever tell you where they were before they came to live in Mile End Road?'

'That they did. Said they'd lived nearer 'Centre' but wanted to live in country when Arthur retired.'

'You don't know if they went to church?'

'Regular as clockwork, every Sunday. St Lukes. That's 'bout a mile along the road back towards 'Centre'.'

'Your husband here today?' Sasha asked for no particular reason.

'No luv. 'enry passed away more'n five year back. Asbestosis it were.'

'Oh, I'm sorry.'

'No need luv. Compensation for that was right generous.'

'Thank you for your help Mrs.........?'

'Stokes, luv.'

'Thank you Mrs Stokes,' and Sasha went back to the Mini, did a three point turn in the road and drove back to the Woodford's house. The house had an estate agent's 'For Sale' sign outside nailed to the wooden fence. When the police had searched the house they had found no Will or documents relating to children and there had been no response to requests in the local and national Press for relatives to get in touch.

It wasn't difficult for Sasha to pick the lock on the back door to enter the house. She spent an hour searching places which the police might have missed and then left, securing the house once more. The lack of family photos, letters, documents and a Will was surprising. If the Woodfords and the others on the package tour were sleepers or agents, she would have expected to find material which would authenticate a false background. Sasha returned to the Mini and drove back along Mile End Road until she found St Lukes. She went into the church and headed for a door to the left of the single step to the chancel which looked as though it might lead to the vestry. Before she was half way down the nave, the vestry door opened and a dog-collared vicar appeared.

'May I help you?' was offered by the vicar.

'Yes if you would.' Sasha had been toying with the idea of making out that she was doing some research, but faced with a young vicar she decided to play it straight. She produced her BID ID. 'I'm Sasha Lilley.'

'Alec Tremlett, vicar of the parish of East Salford.'

'I wonder if I could see the parish records. I'm following up on the tragic murder of the Woodfords. I believe they were regular parishioners of your church, Reverend Tremlett.'

'Yes they were. Follow me please,' and he led Sasha into the vestry. 'What was it you wanted to see?'

'Could I see the register of deaths from 1920 to 1970 please.'

'Of course.'

The vestry was neat and all the documents were kept

inside glass-fronted cabinets. The vicar opened one cabinet and removed three large leather-bound volumes which he placed on the desk.

'Take your time Miss Lilley. I shall be in the church if you need any help.'

It didn't take Sasha nearly as long as she had feared. It was in the second volume – 1940 to 60 - that she found what she was looking for. On 14th November 1959 the Woodford family – father, mother and two children - had all been killed in a car accident. The children's names were Arthur and Hilda. All four had been cremated so no headstones in a graveyard. Sasha dialled Zoe's cellphone.

'Hi, I've found the evidence I needed and I'm on my way back. Any luck, Zoe?'

'Likewise......the birth certificates for Arthur and Hilda Woodford are missing from the General Register Office in Southport. There are computer records of the births, but the certificates have been removed.'

'Want a lift south?'

'Yes please.'

'I'll pick you up at the station. Same place I dropped you. Bye,' and Sasha ended the call.

CHAPTER 26

'Before my team continues with its investigation of Faraway Travel and its clients, sir, I believe that we now have enough useful information to pass on to the agents in Russia,' Fiona Ransby told Mike Carrington in response to his phone call.

'That's a quick result. Well done. I expect the boss would like to listen in on what your team has discovered. I'll bring him down and be with you in five minutes.' In more like three minutes both BID's Director and the Director CE arrived in the team office of CE4.

'I'm going to ask Sasha to give you her information first, sir, because I believe that what she discovered could well be the pattern for the other package tour tourists who were murdered.'

'Thank you, go ahead Sasha,' Miles encouraged.

'The Woodfords really only had one neighbour who lived about a hundred yards from them. This was a Mr and Mrs Stokes. The husband died five years ago. Mrs Stokes told me that the Woodfords kept themselves to themselves, went to church every Sunday and to Russia every year on holiday. In their church, in a very orderly vestry with immaculate records, I discovered that in November 1959, Arthur and Hilda Woodford, aged just three and one, were both killed with their parents in a car accident. Zoe discovered that the birth certificates for both the children had been removed from the General Register Office at Southport. Ryan found nothing at the Criminal Record Board relating to the Woodfords. That's it for me, sir.'

'Thank you Sasha. Who's next Fiona?' Miles Thomson asked.

'Tony Baines, sir.'

'Right, Tony, let's hear what you found.'

'Fortunately, there was a very talkative girl at the travel agent who was very happy to tell me all about the agency. It is a bona fide travel agent, but is acting as a cover for another activity.'

'How did you pick that up?' Mike Carrington asked.

'Luck, sir; a customer was served ahead of me and never said a word to the girl at the counter. She just removed a card from her purse and put it in front of the girl who immediately told her where she was going and the dates of the package. I managed to get a look at the card - it was a Faraway Travel Privilege Card with a seven figure ID number on it.'

'The girl serving her told me that she had no idea how people acquired the cards except that they were very special. There is a dedicated site on the Faraway computers where the girls enter the seven figure number and all the rest is automatic including deducting the payment from the client's account. She went on to say that while she had been with the agency no one had ever applied for a card.'

'All the girls serving were Brits, but their female supervisor was almost certainly Russian or very East European. The girls are trained at the Manchester branch of the agency and each has to act as a tour courier once a year.'

'And your assessment, Tony?' Miles asked.

'An excellent cover for a network of cells and sleepers - or active agents - throughout Europe and the the US - and possibly further afield. An intriguing system, sir, but executed in a rather amateurish fashion. I would not rate this an FSB operation - not professional enough.'

'Thank you Tony. Sasha, what's your assessment?'

'I go along with Tony, sir. There was nothing in the Woodford's house to authenticate their cover; no photographs, no Will, no letters......nothing.'

'Right, so what have we got? Sleepers in this and other countries who receive their instructions or deliver their reports at least once each year by going on a package tour holiday in Russia. This is coordinated by the branches of Faraway Travel. So why are the Russians doing this? Apart from the obvious conclusion of espionage, is it political, military, commercial or some form of subversion? More investigation is needed I think, Mike,' Miles summarised, 'but there is some very useful intelligence that your team has gathered and that should be sent to Gunn and Barnes. Thank you all for that,' and Miles left CE4's office and returned to the 12th floor.

*

'Right John, when you've finished securing our latest captive, we'll place each of them in a separate room. Make sure you tie them to something like this,' and Doyle pointed to a very solid pipe leading to a cast iron radiator. Gunn and Tanya returned and reported that the captives had been secured in the four bedrooms on the first floor.

Gunn's cellphone buzzed with receipt of a text.

'This is an update on Faraway Travel and its customers. The Woodfords were certainly Russian or Russian-recruited sleepers. Very likely that other murdered tourists were also sleepers. Faraway Travel is operating an espionage network across Europe and North America, but no intel as yet for what purpose. Rayner's death was not suicide. He was murdered by his PA.'

Gunn showed the text to the other two. 'Before we question the four upstairs I think it's time we learnt from you, Tanya, what the boss told you and how much you know about this lot.'

CHAPTER 27

'A considerable amount because I was briefed by the head of the UK cell of this Russian espionage network,' Tanya replied.'

'Rayner?' Gunn queried which brought a chuckle from Tanya.

'Rayner was a pawn....a high-placed pawn, but nothing more than that. The head of the UK operation is Taisia Barkov.......'

'Tricia Baker?'

'Just so.'

'BID's boss know that?' Doyle asked.

'He's suspected it for some time, but was unable to find the proof he needed to close down the cell and all its tentacles. That's why he agreed to send me to Russia ahead of you.'

'So what's the aim of this.....network?' Doyle asked, 'and do you have any leads on the CIA cell?'

'Yes, but not quite as clear cut as the BID cell. I'm pretty certain that your Head of NCS is a key player, but like BID he's not the boss. Does he have a female Deputy?'

'Sure, she has the same pay grade security clearance as Merton,' Doyle replied.

'Her name?' Tanya asked.

'Gilian Lawson.'

'Rayner spoke of a 'Galina Lapayev' who is the KKS asset in the USA.'

'KKS?' both men queried.

'I'll come to that in a minute.'

'And the network?' Doyle asked.

'Ah yes......it was set up in 1991 as the Berlin Wall and the Soviet Union collapsed. Its founder was Major Vasily Zhukov who developed the network initially to help Colonel General Yuri Volkonoff - star KGB interrogator - trade nuclear warheads with Muammar Gaddafi and Saddam Hussein. Warheads supposedly destroyed under the terms of the Strategic Arms Limitation Treaty.'

'Does the network have a name?' Gunn asked.

'Komitet za Kommercheskii Shpionazh - operates under the acronym of KKS. You guys will know that as the Committee for Commercial Espionage. Oh, and Zhukov has promoted himself to Colonel,' Tanya added.'

'Yea, we picked that up from the recorded message he left us over the road. Do you know where he's gone and how he planned to get there?' Doyle asked.

'There was a Zil 4x4 parked at this house yesterday' Tanya replied. 'I expect Zhukov will have used that to go to the airport where he has a helicopter. That's the only way to get to the gulag. Rayner told me that Zhukov has a deputy.....Georgy Balashov....he is a particularly unpleasant piece of work. He was here until last night so he must have gone with Zhukov. What do you plan on doing with these four?'

'That depends a great deal on what we learn from questioning them,' Doyle replied.

'Did you pick up anything about this informer who we're supposed to meet at the station?' Gunn asked.

'No.....nothing. It was never mentioned during the time I was with them. This is what you want,' and Tanya dug a small piece of paper out of her jeans pocket and handed it to Gunn. 'Those are the Latitude and Longitude coordinates of the gulag where Zhukov has gone and, presumably, where

Peter and Ben have been taken.'

Gunn unfolded the paper. On it were the coordinates:

North 50°46'27.85" East 137°35'11.36"

'Zhukov said he'd come and collect me as soon as he had set up the exchange of agents with the CIA and BID.'

Gunn decided there was no point in asking Tanya how she had managed to get the coordinates.

'Half-an-hour to mid-day; I think it's time we kept that RV at the station,' Gunn said looking at his watch.

CHAPTER 28

'Eighteen minutes to go,' Doyle announced to the other two in the Gaz after checking his watch. 'Have you got those directions to the station Tanya gave us?'

'Yes.....here,' and Gunn pulled the slip of paper out of his pocket. 'Take a right and then a left in about 400 yards and then straight on over the railway and the station should be on your right.'

'Got it. Any idea at all who or what we might be looking for at the station?' Doyle addressed his question to both Gunn and Tanya.

'Apart from the recorded message stating that the informant would be in the station concourse, I have no idea what to expect. You John?' Tanya asked.

'The message said that the "informant would be there at mid-day", but nothing about how long he....or she, would be there or, for that matter, if it was a person at all,' Gunn offered and then continued. 'I mean what are we expecting? Some sort of indication where this scientist, Chong, is holed up or the location of the gulags - which Tanya has already provided.'

'I was hoping it might be where this Chong guy was hiding.....but perhaps that's overly simple,' Doyle suggested as he executed a quick right and left and headed for the bridge over the tracks.

'Not at all. I think that's what we , the CIA and BID are all hoping, but I'm juggling with some lateral thinking just in case there's a nasty or......highly unlikely....a nice surprise in store for us. Ever the optimist,' Gunn concluded.

'No, that makes sense. So what else could it be?' Tanya floated the question from the back of the Gaz. Each of them suggested various options which varied from absolutely nothing to an ambush by the FSB or the KKS. This kept them occupied as they approached the station.

Doyle followed the signs to the car park at the station where he was greeted by a large parking area which was nearly empty and where the parking was free.

'Right guys how do we play this one?' Tanya asked as they all got out of the Gaz. Gunn looked at his watch.

'Five minutes to go. We split up now and head for the station entrance and concourse, but we keep each other in view the whole time. If nothing has happened by three minutes after mid-day we meet back at the car - still keeping each other in view. OK? Any other ideas?' Gunn asked.

'You two guys are considerably taller than all the people around this part of Russia,' Tanya pointed out. 'Both of you will stick out like a sore thumb. Not only that, but if there is a sniper or whatever, both of you will make an easier target. Let me make the contact. Does that all make sense?'

'Yes it does. I'll dial your cellphone now so that I can warn you if I spot anything. Right?' Gunn hit the speed dial on his cellphone which Tanya answered and then replaced it in her anorak pocket. 'Anything else?' Both Doyle and Tanya shook their heads. 'Right, let's go.'

They split up and headed for the very grand station entrance. Tanya was more used to the splendour that the Russians devoted to the architecture of their public buildings, but both Doyle and Gunn were hardly expecting the grandeur of the concourse in which they arrived via the imposing entrance. The concourse was mostly white marble with pillars scattered along its length and lit by elegant chandeliers. It was far more like a Tsarist palace than a Soviet era train station.

Gunn looked at his watch. Two minutes to mid-day. The concourse was fairly crowded, but mostly by shoppers rather than travellers as it was filled with retail outlets like an airport departure lounge. One minute to mid-day. The PA system was announcing the arrival of the BAM express in both Russian and English.

The minute hand of the large ornate analogue clock with four faces hanging from the ceiling in the centre of the concourse clicked up to the 12 to join the hour hand......mid-day. The announcement about the arrival of the express ceased.

"Will the tourist meeting Mr Chong Yejoon please go to the information desk in the centre of the concourse opposite platform three where there is a message for him."

Unlike most station PA systems in the UK, the announcement was clear and articulate and repeated twice in English.

'What d'you reckon?' Tanya asked on her cellphone.

'I'm only twenty yards from the information desk. There are about ten people there. Go towards it now, but try and keep people around you. If I shout, drop to the ground,' Gunn warned.

Doyle had moved closer to Tanya. She had bought herself a bag of sweets and was in the process of unwrapping one of them. There were three girls behind the desk, dressed in BAM's smart uniform of navy blue jackets and skirts, white shirts and red-top peaked caps. Tanya was amongst a small group of people at the information desk.

'Had this announcement been repeated day after day since 4th July?' Gunn wondered. His eyes scanned every possible place around the concourse from which a sniper might get a clear shot at someone standing at the information desk. It had been a situation very similar to this on his last assignment that Tanya had saved his life by spotting an assassin in the crowd on Berlin's Hauptbahnhof.

'Crack and thump'; the crack came first and that was the bullet breaking the sound barrier as it sped past you - you hoped. Then the thump: the detonation of the cartridge that had fired the bullet. That's what you had to identify because that told you where the sniper was. That's what his Small Arms School instructors had taught him.

While keeping one eye on Tanya at the information desk, Gunn scanned the concourse for possible sniper positions; within split seconds he spotted a dozen places which would offer a commanding view of anyone at the information desk. There was a mezzanine level on three sides of the concourse with more retail outlets and a cafe. One of the shops on the mezzanine even specialised in hunting gear, clothing and what looked like scoped rifles from where Gunn was standing. The mezzanine was the only area from where someone could get a clear shot at a target standing at the information desk.

Why would someone or some organisation go to to all the trouble of getting the message to the CIA about the survivors of Flight 007 and then assassinate the person sent by the intelligence agency? Had the three of them got this all wrong? Gunn wondered as he scanned the mezzanine.

There were three.......or was it four people sitting outside the mezzanine cafe, Gunn turned away from Tanya to check. They were all standing up and moving away from the cafe. About to board the BAM train which had just arrived? No......it seemed as though the cafe was closing. Why close just after mid-day?

'Get ready to duck!' Gunn said into his cellphone.

Tanya's nod indicated that she had got the message. She was now standing in front of the middle girl of the three at the desk. Gunn was barely five yards from her and Doyle the same distance on the other side.

'Dobroe utr........izvinite, khorosho eer dnem,' the BAM receptionist apologised for the 'good morning' and changed it to 'good afternoon'.

'Oh, hi there, I'm the tourist meeting Mr Chong Yejoon. You've just called me on the PA system. I believe there's a..........'

Crack!

CHAPTER 29

Thump!

Chaos at the information desk......some people screaming, others in tears and yet another man retching into a litter bin. Blood, bone, brain matter, hair, scalp and pieces of skull splattered all over the display panel at the back of the information desk.

Tanya was on her knees in front of the desk. She had dropped to a kneeling position. Gunn had clearly heard the 'thump', but so had Doyle who was quicker than him. Gunn saw him sprinting across the concourse towards the escalator leading up to the mezzanine level. The exploding RDX-tipped bullet had decapitated the young girl who had greeted Tanya. Her headless, blood soaked trunk was still sitting in the chair. People were running in every direction, but mostly away from the information desk.

Another shot.....but Gunn was sure that came from an automatic and sounded very like Doyle's Smith and Wesson .45 automatic. Doyle was now running towards the mezzanine escalator, followed by Gunn. No sign of any police yet as people streamed out of the station into the car park. There was a shout from someone on the mezzanine level. Another shot....then more shouting. Gunn and Doyle took the moving steps of the 'up' escalator two at a time whilst other shoppers and travellers fought to get on the 'down' escalator and away from whatever was happening on the mezzanine level.

Gunn caught a glimpse of Doyle at the far end of the mezzanine level where a spiral staircase led up to what could be a maintenance walkway on the roof of the station. Doyle reached the stairs first and raced up them quickly followed by Gunn. As they reached the roof, the sniper stepped off the metal walkway and started running across the shallow-pitched, green-tiled roof of the station. The sniper rifle had been discarded and the man was now carrying a handgun. As he reached the apex of the roof he turned and raised the automatic to fire at Doyle who was only a few yards behind him.

Gunn fired twice.....a long shot......40 or 50 yards. The sniper's gun hand slowly dropped to his side and the gun clattered onto the tiled roof. He sank to his knees and then fell over onto the pitched roof before rolling all the way down to where Gunn was standing. He ended up face down in the guttering on the edge of the roof beside the walkway.

Gunn bent and turned him over onto his back.

'That's Balashov,' Tanya said breathlessly, having just caught up with the two men.

*

'Thompson.'

'Ops Centre, sir, Terry Holt. Text message from John Gunn.'

'On my way,' and Miles Thompson replaced his phone, said 'ops centre' to Angela his PA as he passed her door and took the stairs two at a time to the 14th floor.

The Operations Centre on the 14th floor functioned 24/7 for 365 days a year. It was operated by its permanent staff during the hours of 9 to 5 and then by duty staff from both E and CE Directorates of BID. Terry Holt, the Controller of the Ops Centre had a work station that was almost as high tech as NASA's Mission Control at Houston. He controlled his empire from a raised platform in the centre of the room from where he could see every operator and the various screens, VDUs and displays which could be programmed to cover every city, town or village in the UK or any country in the World with a K-Band data link to the satellites and Unmanned Aerial Vehicles (UAVs) being controlled from Langley.

As BID's Director reached the central podium, Terry handed him a copy of Gunn's text:

Carried out the RV at 1200 today. Contact was a message over the station PA system for person meeting Chong Yejoon to go to information desk. This was done but we became target for sniper. Sniper's bullet killed the girl at the reception desk but meant for us. Pursued sniper onto roof of station. Sniper shot by us. Sniper was Balashov who is Zhukov's deputy. Now on run from Russian police. Heading for gulags unless directed otherwise by EDS.

'Please send to Gunn - From Managing Director Express Delivery Service. Proceed as planned.' Miles returned the text message to Terry Holt and left the Ops Centre.

CHAPTER 30

In addition to the spiral steel stairway access to the roof from the mezzanine, there were metal rungs let into the walls of the station at either end of the maintenance walkway on the roof. The three of them climbed down the rungs on the side of the building facing away from the car park as sirens heralded the arrival of the police. Resisting the urge to run, they walked round to the front of the station and headed for the Gaz. With Doyle in the driver's seat, they reversed out of the parking slot and drove out of the car park barely moments ahead of two policemen who placed cones across the car park access to prevent any other cars from either entering or leaving it. Gunn's cellphone rang. He took the call and then turned to the other two.

'Whoever it was who attempted to shoot Tanya has scuppered any hope of finding whatever it was we were supposed to discover from the contact at the information desk. If it was more detailed information about the location of Chong then that's been lost. I have to say Tanya it seems as though Zhukov has been been playing a double or even tripple game. Hardly surprising. He has his two hostages which he will use as bargaining chips for the CIA's Galina Lapayev and BID's Taisia Barkov. I think Balashov was given the task of killing you, Tanya. I suggest we go back to Malinkovskaya Street and see what's happened there. BID has cleared us to go to the gulag to either prove or disprove the recorded message about Chong Yejoon. What about the CIA?' Gunn asked Doyle who was studying his cellphone with half an eye while keeping the other on the mid-day traffic in Khabarovsk.

'Likewise....approval to continue. What can we expect at the Malinkovskaya house?'

'Much as we left it........unless there are more of Zhukov's guys,' Tanya offered, 'but can I offer a word of caution.'

'Go ahead,' Gunn encouraged.

'There is something odd about the four people in that house - Slava, Ilya, Alexei and Irena. I had known them for only a short time and they accepted me because presumably Zhukov – the self-styled Assassin - had been briefed by either Rayner or Taisia Barkov....the latter more likely. Balashov was creepy and was always watching me. But those other four are weird.....'

'Weird, in what way?' Doyle asked and then added, 'nearly there guys.'

'They appear to be either brain-washed or in some other form of zombie like state. If there is any truth in this conspiracy theory about the survivors of that Korean Boeing 747 then it might just be that these are evidence of that theory, but that's unlikely as they can't be older than their mid twenties and it's nearly thirty years since that incident. If they are still there then can I suggest we handle with care.'

'Agreed,' from Gunn. There was no further conversation until Doyle pulled into the right side of the street fifty yards short of the house they had left just an hour earlier that morning for the station RV.

They got out of the car and crossed over to the left side of the street. Gunn turned to Doyle.

'Can you take the back.'

'Sure,' and Doyle moved away from the other two to get round the side of the house.

'Tanya, can you stay a couple of yards behind me to cover me from any activity from the first floor windows.'

'OK,' and she moved into position as Gunn went up to the front door of the house with the Glock held ready for instant use if required.

The front door was ajar. Gunn pushed it open with his foot. Not a sound anywhere.....and then a shout from the first floor. As Gunn went to the stairs Tanya moved into the house behind him to cover him. The first door he opened revealed the woman, Irena.

'Tualet pozhaluista!' she pleaded in Russian to be allowed to go to the toilet.

'Knife needed asp!' Gunn shouted down to Tanya who appeared moments later with a kitchen knife.

'Poor woman's desperate for the loo.....over to you!' and Gunn left Irena in Tanya's care while he went to the next bedroom. Doyle appeared at this juncture and together they cut the cable ties securing Slava, Alexei and Ilya to the bedroom plumbing and escorted them downstairs to the lounge. Irena reappeared with Tanya and then the three men asked to use the toilet. Once all the toilet procedure was finished, the four of them were told to sit on the sofa. Gunn had suggested that Tanya start the questioning as both her Japanese and her Russian were native fluent and they were more likely to trust her than Gunn and Doyle.

Ethnically, the three seemed to be more like Asians than Russians, but from the experience of his previous assignment Gunn knew that little significance could be attached to that because a large proportion of the inhabitants of Eastern Russia had the same ethnic appearance.

'Annyeonghaseyo,' - good afternoon - Tanya addressed the three people on the sofa in Korean without warning. Yet another language that she speaks fluently no doubt, Gunn thought. The three looked at her and hesitantly repeated the greeting.

'Sorry, that's the limit of my Korean, but they certainly knew what I said.' Tanya switched to Russian and questioned them for nearly and hour before she paused and glanced at Gunn.

'I expect you got all of that, but now you can see what seems so odd. Not one of these three can remember anything about their childhood. They don't know where they were born or anything about their parents and Slava and Ilya have no idea of their age. Irena and Alexei think that they are 21 or 22. The only thing they can remember is living in a gulag in the Taiga. All four appear to be brain-washed Koreans which perhaps supports the conspiracy theory that some or all of the passengers on the KAL flight survived the crash in 1983.'

CHAPTER 31

'So what do we do with them?' Tanya asked, switching from Russian to English. Slava, Alexei, Ilya and Irena had lapsed into what appeared to be a trance, displaying what appeared to be the symptoms of hypnosis.

'They seem pretty harmless, but we can't just leave them here,' Doyle replied studying the four silent stooges that the Assassin had brought with him from the gulag. Before Doyle got any further with his suggestions he was interrupted by Gunn who had been looking out of the window which fronted onto the street.

'We've run out of time guys. There are soldiers in the street outside moving from cover to cover and taking up fire positions.....probably doing the same at the back of this house. Whoever Balashov was, he must have contacted the military command in this area before he tried to deal with us at the station. Tanya, can you tell our silent friends what's happening and ask them if they know of any magic to get us out of here.......preferably alive.'

The moment that Tanya addressed the trio the reaction was exactly as though she had flicked a switch. All three became focused, but some of the hurried Russian conversation was too fast for both Gunn and Doyle. Tanya finished speaking to the four Russians who immediately got up and headed for the kitchen at the back of the house.

'No magic guys, but this house does have a purpose-built escape route - not unusual for any part of Russia where they've lived in fear of repression and families disappearing in dawn raids since the Revolution. They've told me to follow them so it looks like we take them with us.....for the time being anyway. Anyone got a better idea?' Tanya asked as she picked up her small backpack and followed the Russianss. Doyle and Gunn followed Tanya into the kitchen.

In the far corner of the kitchen was a larder built against an outside wall where it would benefit from the cold to keep food fresh. At the back of the larder was a wall full of shelves filled with metal containers and glass jars. This wall opened outwards revealing a black rectangular opening in the floor. Irena had already disappeared into the opening followed by Slava, Alexei and Ilya. Gunn reached for a torch in the bottom of his pack, but at that moment the opening in the floor was filled with light; the escape route had its own illumination. Doyle was just disappearing into the opening when a splintering crash signalled the arrival of the soldiers in the house. He slid the rest of the way down the ladder as Gunn climbed down closing the false wall of the larder behind him.

The tunnel was brick-lined and the two men at the rear only had to stoop slightly to walk along it. There was a strong smell of sewage which gave all of them an idea of where this escape route was heading. In only twenty or thirty yards there was a sharp right bend and then the tunnel floor sloped down in a series of steps until it opened out into a main sewer. The stench was overpowering, but preferable to whatever was behind them in the house on Malinkovskaya Street. Irena said something to Tanya who turned to Gunn and Doyle.

'We'll need our torches now,' she announced.

Once they were were all in the main sewer, Slava reached into a cavity in the tunnel wall. The lights in the tunnel went out followed by a medieval dungeon-like sound of iron clanking on stone.

'The tunnel is now blocked by an iron grill,' Slava informed them.

Guided by the light from the torches they followed the Russian trio along the sewer. The floor of the sewer was concrete with a channel in the middle for the sewage. The walls were curved and constructed of brick. They were walking along the concrete floor which was treacherously slippery with a slimy deposit not helped by scores of large, sleek rats which scurried over their feet.

'Shit!' a muted oath from Doyle as he almost lost his balance on the slimed concrete.

'That's it in a word,' Gunn chuckled from behind him.

'I swear, John, I'll never ever be rude about guys who work in these sewers........hold on, looks as though we've reached a major junction of the sewage system.'

Their sewer opened out into a vaulted confluence of other sewers. Their torches couldn't illuminate the extent of the underground gallery, but their three guides walked nimbly over various channels until they reached an iron ladder cemented into the brickwork and reaching up into the darkness above them. Tanya turned round.

'They say we are now several streets away from Malinkovskaya and if we don't leave the sewer here the next opportunity is the outflow into the Amur River......another mile or so further on. Decision?'

'Leave here!' Gunn and Doyle said in unison.

CHAPTER 32

At the top of the ladder was a cast iron cover which Slava and Ilya had removed. The sewer access was in the middle of a residential road, fortunately with only an occasional car using it at that time in the early evening. The two Russians directed the traffic around the open sewer cover while Alexei, Irena, Tanya, Doyle and Gunn emerged into the street, everyone gulping in breaths of fresh sewer-free air.

'Rather like garlic,' Gunn muttered while the Russians replaced the cover. 'Just as well we all stink of sewage.' The six escapees from the Malinkovskaya house moved off the road onto the pavement. Their appearance out of a sewer access had attracted little attention, but the speed of the military raid on the house had left them no time to make any plans to continue the search for Peter Samarin and Ben Warren. 'How did the four of you get here from the gulag?' Gunn addressed the Russianss who had led them out of the Malinkovskaya house.

'We came in a helicopter with Colonel Zhukov and Major Balashov,' Slava replied.

'Is there any other way of getting to the gulag other than by helicopter?' Gunn asked.

'There used to be a rough, unsealed road which led off the main highway in Khurmuli, but that has not been used for many years and by now will have returned to taiga,' this information came from Ilya.

'OK, so that rules out any option other than a helicopter. Can you remember where you landed in the helicopter?' Gunn asked.

'Oh yes, that was at Novy Airport, but the only helicopters near here are at Garovka Air Force Base.'

'And where is that?'

'It's to the north-east of the city very close to the city's Novy Airport. There are buses that go out to the airport and the Air Base,' came from Irena and before Gunn could ask she continued. 'The buses leave from the station every twenty minutes. I speak a little English and I know that you are wondering what to do with us. I have spoken with my friends while we were down there,' she pointed with her foot at the sewer manhole cover in the road, 'and we have all agreed that we would like to help you find your friends who were taken by Colonel Zhukov. We could be useful to you as we know the gulag, but if you don't want that you can leave us here and we will try to start a new life.'

'Thanks Irena, I will now speak to my friends,' and Gunn turned to Doyle and Tanya. In unison they said, 'take them with us'.

'That's settled then.....bus or taxi? Fortunately we have plenty of roubles, but I vote for a bus.'

'A taxi driver will remember us. A bus is better as long as the other passengers can put up with the smell,' came from Doyle.

'I assume you guys are planning to take a chopper from the Air Base.....correct?' Tanya asked.

'Correct,' from Gunn.

'Presumably you will do that when it's dark?'

'Makes sense,' Doyle offered.

'It won't be dark for some time yet so why don't we find a hotel, clean ourselves up and do our planning in comfort?'

'Agreed, let's ask our Russian friends if they know a low-key hotel where we won't attract too much attention.'

The advice from the three Russians was to go to the Chaika Airport Hotel which they said was used to tourists checking in for just a few hours. Neither Gunn nor Doyle decided to pursue the enquiry but both wondered just how long the Russians had been in Khabarovsk before Tanya had met up with them. Like any group of tourists they hailed a couple of taxis after walking towards the city centre for ten minutes. Gunn took the lead taxi with Slava and Irena and Doyle followed with Tanya, Alexei and Ilya.

They had no difficulty reserving two rooms; Tanya and Irena in one room and the men in the other. Gunn and Doyle made sure that one of them was always with the other two men, but neither gave any inclination to do anything other than follow instructions which confirmed Gunn's suspicion that they had either been brain-washed or hypnotised.

Khabarovsk shares the same Latitude as London, which meant that in July it did not get fully dark until after ten in the evening. Washed, refreshed and with clothes aired, they were all considerably better prepared for the next phase of the search for Ben and Peter which required the theft of a helicopter from a Russian air base with all the risks that that involved, followed by a 400 mile flight over the taiga to find the gulag.

It would be a toss-up to guess what helicopters, would be at the air base. Alexei and Ilya said that they had seen helicopters landing there but were unable to be specific about what they had seen. Both Gunn and Doyle were qualified to fly a number of helicopters; Doyle more than Gunn as he had taken part in the Red Flag exercises in the Nevada desert where almost every type of Russian aircraft and helicopter, retrieved from various parts of the World, added authenticity to the training of US and NATO fast-jet pilots.

The hotel reception had provided Gunn with a map of the area on which the Garovka Air Force Base was shown. The plan was simple. Gunn and Doyle would walk the two miles to the Base and get past the security by whatever means. They would then have to find a fully-fuelled helicopter and fly it back to the hotel car park where they would land and pick up Tanya and the four Russians. Communication between Tanya and the two men would be by cellphone. The simplicity of the plan covered a myriad of things that could and probably would go wrong. There was neither time for, nor any sense in a 'recce' of the airbase. In Russia, anyone wandering around in the proximity of an operational air base would instantly result in arrest, or death.

CHAPTER 33

While Ilya, Alexei and Slava were showering, Gunn and Doyle emptied out the contents of their packs onto the double bed. In addition to the two automatics which both carried, their controllers had brought out a number of basic survival aids in the diplomatic bag.

These items had included the torches which had been invaluable in the sewer, bushcraft knives, fishing line and hooks, short chrome-steel crowbars, stun, smoke and fragmentation grenades, cable-ties, Duck tape, flints for fire-lighting, morphine syrettes in a first aid kit, binoculars, compass, maps printed on silk, GPS and a guide of what could and could not be eaten in the wild to survive. What they had laid out on the bed was duplicated in Tanya's backpack. The hotel had a cafeteria restaurant which served food 24/7. They all ate and by 9.30pm, fed and rested, Gunn and Doyle decided it was dark enough for them to set off on the walk to the air force base.

Before they left, they took the five who were remaining at the hotel out to the car park where they agreed the exact LZ for the helicopter to pick them up. Gunn told Tanya that if the whole escapade went 'tits-up' and either he and Doyle were killed or arrested or they discovered that there were no choppers at all, none suitable or there was a danger of them starting World War Three, then they would meet back at the hotel and have a rethink.

Once they had left the outskirts of the airport, there was no traffic on what the map supplied by the hotel showed as the road to the air base. Only two vehicles passed them - one in each direction - and the loom from their headlights gave the two men plenty of time to crouch out of sight in the scrub on the roadside. After ten minutes brisk walk they saw the lights of the air force base and from that point on they left the road and walked through the low scrub. The natural flora of the taiga - conifers with a mix of birch, alder, willow and poplar - had all been cleared from an area extending 200 yards out from the 10 foot high steel-fenced perimeter of the base. Many of the trees had re-sprouted providing the two men with perfect cover and the thick moss and lichen on the ground absorbed any noise of their approach.

Without a recce of the base or any prior knowledge of it, they had to assume it possessed the highest level of security - if that wasn't the case, then so much the better. Fifty yards from the main entrance to the base they stopped and both studied the guardhouse, the gates and the military personnel guarding the access to the base through their binoculars. It was a mild evening and the guards were walking about, chatting and smoking - the first indication that the supervision of the guards was slack.

'I don't think these guys can be expecting anything to disturb their peaceful stag on guard duty,' Gunn said quietly.

'Don't suppose much happens in this eastern extremity of the Russian Federation. The only time that this area of Russia hit the headlines was when they shot down that KAL flight back in '83.' And then Doyle added, 'they've got CCTV at the gate, but I can't see any other cameras. You?'

'No, but doesn't mean there aren't any......careful, there's a vehicle coming.'

In fact there were two vehicles. The first was a Gaz jeep - almost a carbon copy of the US Willys jeep of World War 2 fame. The jeep was followed by a Maz 537 tank transporter, but instead of a tank on its low-loader trailer, it had the damaged fuselage of a helicopter, partially covered by a tarpaulin.

'C'mon buddy, this is our ticket into the base,' and as the slow moving Maz ground past the two men, Doyle jumped to his feet and ran across to the low-loader trailer followed by Gunn. They climbed onto the trailer and Doyle went to the sliding door on their side of the fuselage, pushed back the catch in the recessed aperture and slid open the door. They both climbed in and closed the door.

'We're in luck if they've got these on the base,' Doyle said with no need to lower his voice as the noise made by the Maz tractor drowned all other noise. 'This is a Kamov K60......almost a direct copy of your British Westland Lynx chopper. If they've got these on the base we're in luck. Got a range of about 500 miles, a max speed of nearly 200 mph and can carry about a dozen armed soldiers in this compartment. It's got dual control in the cockpit as the Ruskies use it for training their chopper pilots.'

The jeep and low-loader barely paused at the gate to the base and no one bothered to check either of the vehicles. Once they were clear of the lax security at the gate the two men climbed cautiously out of the Kamov. The low-loader was heading towards the far side of the base where there were rows of Antonov transport aircraft and at least twenty similar Kamovs to the one on the low loader.

'Now all we have to do is pray that all the choppers are fully fuelled,' Gunn said as he studied the buildings closest to the Kamov helicopters. Gunn's prayer was answered. There was a fuel tanker parked up by one of the Kamov helicopters and ground crew were in the process of refuelling it. Gunn and Doyle dropped off the side of the low-loader and headed for a building which looked as though it was a crew room. No one took any notice of them. Initially this surprised the two men but they then realised that there were a number of men in that area in both uniform, flying overalls and civilian mufti so two more with backpacks over one shoulder caused no interest.

'What d'you reckon, John.......about to go on a mission or just returned and being refuelled,' Doyle asked nodding towards the Kamov being re-fuelled.

'My guess would be about to go on a mission......here, this looks promising,' and Gunn led the way through an entrance into what was obviously a tasking centre and crew room area. Two men in flying overalls were walking towards them. There was no time to avoid them. Gunn turned to Doyle and spoke in Russian.

'I tell you Igor I reckon that both those two tarts in the bar were on the game. What do you reckon?'

'Might've been Nikolai, but I didn't fancy yours.'

They both laughed and greeted the two airmen as they passed. The greeting was returned without any interest taken in the two men in mufti.

CHAPTER 34

Gunn had kept an eye on the door from which the two air crew had emerged. The door was identified as 'Crew Changing Room' in Cyrillic script - 'EKIPAZH RAZDEVALKE'. He opened the door which revealed an area of steel lockers, changing rooms, toilets and shower facilities. The room was empty. The two men closed the door behind them and put their packs on the wooden benches. All the steel lockers were locked, but a quick examination revealed that it would require no great effort to force the doors.

'Look for some overalls and helmets?' Gunn queried.

'Yeah, why not,' Doyle replied, removing the steel crowbar from his backpack. The first locker he opened revealed overalls to fit a pilot no taller than 5'6" and almost as broad. He opened three more before he found one which fitted. Gunn was successful on his second attempt. They removed their anoraks which they stuffed into their packs and pulled on the overalls. They had only just finished when the door opened and three men in uniform entered. Having closed all the lockers with forced locks they held their breath, but with a muttered, 'dobryi vecher', the three men went to another row of lockers. They returned the greeting of 'good evening' and left the changing room. Diagonally across the corridor from the changing room was another sign for the 'Crew Room' - again in Cyrillic script - 'EKIPAZH KOMNATE'.

'Hell, luck's on our side. Let's give it a go,' and Doyle pushed the door open and entered the crew room. It was just like any RAF or US Air Force crew room - easy chairs, hot drink machines, snacks, TV and girly magazines. As they entered, Doyle almost collided with a senior NCO.

'There you are, sir! You must be the pilots returning to Chernigovka Air Force Base with the spare parts for the SU25 bomber,' and before Doyle or Gunn could mutter anything in response, 'they've just finished refuelling your aircraft, the spares have been loaded and air traffic is ready to despatch you.'

'Thank you,' both said in unison and walked out of the door onto the airfield where the Kamov helicopter indicated by the NCO was parked up.

'Jesus, just how lucky can you get,' Doyle said out of the side of his mouth as they walked purposefully to the Kamov. They placed their packs in the passenger compartment and climbed into the cockpit while the ground crewman closed the sliding door and then the two doors on either side of the cockpit.

'Any idea where Chernigovka Air Force Base is?.....I mean just so that it looks as though we are heading in the right direction,' Gunn asked as Doyle pulled on his helmet and plugged in the jack-plug.

'Vaguely.....it's just to the north of Vladivostok, so as long as we head in a southerly direction....which we will do anyway, because that's where we pick up the other guys before we head north-east into the taiga.'

Air traffic control contacted them and gave them flight instructions which Gunn acknowledged for Doyle as his hands went nimbly over the switches. He started the two Rybinsk turboshaft engines and they waited on tenterhooks for the dials to move into the green sectors. While they waited Gunn dialled Tanya's cellphone number and sent a text warning her of their imminent arrival.

'There'll be some protocol for taxying out and taking off which I'll probably get wrong, but let's hope that ATC think that's because we're based at Chernigovka....OK here we go,' and the Kamov moved out of its parking slot onto the taxiway.

'Kamov KA five zero one, control tower.... you are clear for take off,' came over their headsets in Russian. Doyle increased the power with his left hand on the throttle of the collective pitch and right hand on the cyclic pitch as the Kamov rose into the night sky, banked to the left and headed for the airport hotel.

Doyle immediately identified the hotel two miles to the south and the car park to the east side of it. A figure was standing in the agreed LZ flashing a torch.

'That looks like Tanya, but no sign of the other four,' Gunn said.

'It's too late now to worry about them if they've decided to disappear. Can't say I blame them. If I'd been locked up in a gulag for God knows how long I'd be pretty damn keen to stay away,' Doyle answered as he brought the Kamov into the hover over the car park and slowly brought it down onto the tarmac. As the wheels touched, the sliding door was pulled back and Tanya climbed in and pulled the door closed behind her. Gunn reached back and handed her a headset which she put on.

'Just me.......no idea where the other four are. We were all together until I got that text from you and then they said they thought it would be a good idea to have a pee before the flight. No sign of them after that.'

'OK...just the three of us it is,' and Doyle lifted the Kamov off the car park and in a wide sweeping turn to the north-east headed for the co-ordinates of the gulag some 450 miles away in the taiga.

CHAPTER 35

Patrick Merton, Head of the CIA's National Clandestine Service, loaded his golf bag into the back of his Audi station wagon parked in the drive of 24 Springfield Way, Rockville. The neat, white house with its manicured lawns was just six miles away from the CIA Headquarters on the north side of the Potomac River and a couple of miles from the Lakewood Country Club where he was due to meet up with three of his colleagues from the Agency for the customary Saturday morning round of golf.

It was a gorgeous summer's day and he whistled through his teeth as he drove unhurriedly through the plush residential streets to the club. At the club he met up with his three colleagues and the foursome headed out to the first tee. His cellphone vibrated with receipt of a text message. All of them kept their cellphones switched on, but in silent mode. He unlocked the phone and read the text:

'At the second hole, Snakeback, fade your drive into Lake Copse'

'Sorry about that guys,' he apologised, but all of them were used to interruptions to their round of golf and on a number of occasions the round had had to be abandoned when a crisis had developed at the Agency. Patrick was a good golfer with a handicap of eleven and he won the first hole with a birdie three. That was $10 in the kitty for him. He had the honour at the second tee and produced a well crafted fade which bounced in the rough and disappeared into the trees of Lake Copse. There were mutters of 'bad luck' from his colleagues and once all of them had driven off, his buggy partner let him take the buggy to search for his ball. He parked it at the point outside the Copse where the ball had disappeared, armed himself with a sand wedge to beat the undergrowth - and to make the whole charade convincing - and disappeared amongst the trees.

His three colleagues all took their second shots and turned in the direction of the Copse, but there was no sign of Patrick. John Haseman, the Head of Homeland Security and a regular member of the foursome, climbed into the second buggy and headed for the Copse. The remaining two waved on the two-ball following them to play through, but a shout from the Copse had them running in that direction to discover what had happened to Patrick. They pulled the branches aside and headed for John Haseman who was standing, looking down at the body of Patrick Merton. Haseman turned as the others joined him.

'Looks like suicide. He's shot himself in the head. There's the gun,' he added pointing at a small silenced Beretta lying on the ground close to his right hand

'Not sure about that,' Mark Cavendish, the Head of Science and Technology, muttered as he removed the cellphone from Patrick's trouser pocket. He unlocked it and scrolled back to the last text. 'He was murdered,' Mark announced holding up the cellphone for the others to read the text.

*

The pulsing red LED on the telephone set in front of BID's Director alerted him to an incoming encrypted speech. He picked up the telephone and pressed the 'accept' button. The pulsing red LED changed to a steady green and the calling number appeared in the small VDU. It was the Director of the CIA.

'Yes Leon, it's Miles.' The de-encrypted voice of Leon Panetta sounded as though he was standing in the middle of a vast empty hangar.

'Thanks again for letting me know that you have arrested Taisia Barkov and her key role in the KKS cell there in London.'

'Was that helpful in your continuing investigation of the cell in Langley?' Miles Thompson asked.

'Indeed it was. On Saturday, Patrick Merton, our key suspect, was murdered while out golfing with Agency colleagues. It was made to look like suicide, but a text message on his cellphone showed that it was murder. If he'd deleted the text we would still be no wiser, but the message was traced back to a cellphone belonging to Patrick's PA, Gilian Lawson who we now know is Galina Lapayev thanks to the work of our two agents out there in Russia. She is under arrest and being questioned.'

'That's good news and like us you will want to know how far this KKS cell has spread, its purpose and the extent of any damage it has caused,' Miles replied.

'That is happening now, but it proves the success so far of our joint BID/CIA operation in Russia. Whether our guys are able to find our two missing controllers and prove or disprove the rumours about the passengers from the KAL flight remains to be seen.'

'They are on their way now into the taiga to find the gulag from where this Korean scientist is supposed to have escaped. We will keep you posted of any news we get,' Miles assured the CIA Director.

'Likewise and thanks again,' and Leon Panetta ended the secure call.

Miles replaced the telephone and walked through to his PA. 'Angela, would you ask Mike Carrington to come to my office ASAP.'

CHAPTER 36

'Ah, Mike, come in and thanks for such a quick response,' and Miles Thompson indicated a seat to his Counter-Espionage Director.

'Angela rarely leaves any of us in doubt about the level of urgency expected by her boss,' Mike Carrington smiled as he took a seat. Miles left his desk and joined him.

'Both of the teams you put on to investigate the sleepers and Faraway Travel did a quick and excellent job and now I want to strike while the iron's hot. We know from Tanya Kazakova that this Russian cell has a name.......Komitet za Kommercheskii Schpionazh, or KKS. We need to know its purpose and how far it has spread in the UK and USA.......and elsewhere. From Tony Baines we know that the training centre for Faraway Travel is in Manchester. What we really need to get hold of now is the computer records of all the owners of Privilege Membership of Faraway Travel and then bring them all in before there're any more assassinations. Please treat this operation as second priority only to keeping this Country safe from Al Qaeda.'

'Got all that,' and Mike Carrington got up and left the Director's office.

*

'Right, listen up all of you,' Fiona Ransby, the Head of CE4, had walked into the open-plan main office of her Department in BID's Counter-Espionage Directorate. The last to do so, as usual, was Donald Masterson who was permanently welded to his keyboard and array of VDUs. 'Donald, that includes you.' Reluctantly, he removed his headphones and turned towards his boss. 'Firstly, a pat on the back is in order for Tony's and Sasha's teams. That comes from the Director, but he wants more from us and has told our boss that he wants to act quickly before this self-styled Assassin has a chance to murder any more sleepers. The task that we have been given is to find out the extent of this Russian spy cell.......we now have a name for it: the KKS or Kommitet za Kommercheski Shpionazh.......and its purpose.'

'We know that the briefings are done through Faraway Travel which has a training centre in Manchester and travel agents in London, Washington and possibly elsewhere. We also know that these sleepers are Privilege Members of Faraway Travel. We need the names and addresses of every one of those members so that they can all be rounded up simultaneously. Suggestions please,' Fiona concluded.

'We could start at the training centre,' Tony Baines suggested. 'They must have a record there of all the people who have been trained and possibly all the Privilege Members.'

'No need to do that boss,' came from Donald. He had the attention of all his colleagues.

'OK Donald, what have you got?' Fiona asked, well used to his anarchic approach to his job.

'All the information you want is here. I've hacked into the Faraway Travel website and its password protected confidential area. I have to say that it was pretty bloody easy which makes me think that this outfit has nothing to do with either the old KGB or its replacement, the FSB. It would've taken me a bit longer to defeat their firewalls and safeguards. On here you have all the branches of Faraway Travel with the names of the managers and staff.' Donald was turning VDUs towards his colleagues as he spoke. 'And here are all the names and addresses of the Privilege Members. Lastly, I have a list of eight names matched against the cities of London, Washington, Paris, Ontario, Berlin, Madrid, Rome and Stockholm. I suspect that these are active spies rather than sleepers. Any use to you boss?'

CHAPTER 37

'Anyone for coffee and sandwiches?' Tanya offered the two men in the Kamov's cockpit.

'That's service! Do you have a dry martini by any chance?' Doyle asked, jamming the collective lever with his thigh while he sipped the scalding hot coffee. 'Where did you magic this from?'

'I bought a couple of vacuum flasks from one of the retail outlets and the guy at the snack bar filled them with coffee for me and made up the sandwiches. Choice is ham and cheese or ham and cheese....any preferences?'

'Ham and cheese,' was said in unison from the cockpit.

'Good planning Tanya,' Gunn said through a mouthful of sandwich. 'No idea when we might feed again.'

Doyle was flying the Kamov at tree-top height, skimming along the course of the Amur River at no more than 100 feet to avoid appearing on any Russian air-defence radars. Under the full moon, the river provided an excellent flight path to the north-east, free of all obstructions. It also made it much easier for the Kamov to be spotted by any chase aircraft. He handed control of the helicopter over to Gunn while he ate his sandwich and studied the flight charts which the Russian pilots had left in the helicopter.

The Amur River flowed for 700 miles to the north-east of Khabarovsk to its delta in the Sea of Okhotsk in the narrow strait of Amurskiy Liman between the mainland and Sakhalin Island. The coordinates which Tanya had gleaned from Zhukov lay to the east of the river half way along its course to the sea. The coordinates of the gulag - if genuine, Doyle wondered, as he studied the chart - identified an uninhabited area of the taiga about 30 miles south of the railway which ran from the Russian port of Vanino on the east coast until it connected with the Baykal-Amur Mainline railway in Mongolia.

'Thanks John, I have control,' and Doyle took over the Kamov, refreshed with his coffee and sandwich. The Kamov had a maximum speed in level flight of just under 200 mph. It was now maintaining a speed of 170mph which they hoped would get them to their destination in just under two hours.

A shattering roar and violent turbulence threw the Kamov to one side like a rag doll tossed from a pram.

'Shit!,' Doyle shouted, barely audible in the diminishing roar of the re-heated Turmansky turbofan jets. 'They've sent a fucking 'Fencer' after us. You OK Tanya?'

'Fine, I'm strapped in. Fencer?'

'NATO terminology for a Russian Sukkhoi SU24 - capable of Mach 2 and armed with missiles and cannons. 'Suggestions anyone?' Doyle asked as he dived the Kamov down to within a few feet of the river and hugged the left bank which was in the moon's shadow. Gunn was studying the chart. The Sukhoi was climbing and banking to port to make another pass at the Kamov.

'Hang on guys, this time he'll use his canon,' Doyle warned.

The Russian supersonic attack aircraft was now diving straight at the helicopter. The combined approach speed of the two aircraft was somewhere in the region of 1,000 mph. Doyle brought the Kamov to a juddering halt in the hover, tucked up close to the trees on the left bank of the Amur. The deadly incandescent chain of 30 mm canon shells passed harmlessly over the top of the helicopter.

'He'll be ready for that manoeuvre next time,' Gunn said studying the chart. 'Only a couple of miles away there are power pylons crossing the river. If he comes in low behind us ready for you to pull the hover stunt again you might be able to con him into following you under the pylons. Worth a try?'

'Sure, here we go.' and once again the Kamov skimmed forward over the river as the thunder of the jet's engines receded - momentarily. The Kamov was now fast approaching the pylon line suspended over the river. On either side of the pylon line the conifers of the taiga had been cut back fifty metres which had given Doyle an alternative plan to just heading straight for a duck-under the pylon line.

'Hold tight guys. Can't say I've tried this particular stunt before,' Doyle warned.

'Here he comes Doyle......much slower this time and he's deployed his wings from delta to spread.'

'Here goes,' and Doyle dived the Kamov as though he was aiming to go under the power lines. At the very last second, as they reached the edge of the cutting through the taiga, he banked the helicopter hard over to port, side-slipping under the cables with the helicopter's forward momentum and heading up the cleared cutting with the belly of the Kamov scraping over the top of the cleared low scrub.

The Sukhoi pilot made the mistake of trying to copy the Kamov's manoeuvre in an aircraft totally unsuited to stunt flying. Its port spread wing-tip caught the top of the pylon line cart-wheeling the fast jet into the taiga where it erupted in a violent mushroom cloud of vivid orange and red flame as the aviation fuel and ordnance exploded.

'Sorry to be a pessimist, but I expect there'll be another one as they are usually sent to hunt in pairs,' Doyle warned the other two as he turned the Kamov back to the river and continued their flight to the north-east.

CHAPTER 38

'To the east of us, the flight chart shows a spine of high ground stretching all the way from Vladivostok to roughly where we are heading........it calls itself the Sikhole Alin. You might like to try some low level flying amongst the hills which would make us harder to spot,' Gunn suggested as he studied the chart.

'Worth a try,' and Doyle turned the Kamov to starboard and headed for the foothills of the mountain range which had one or two peaks of over 2,000 metres. Only seconds after they had reached the deeply corrugated foothills of the taiga they spotted the second Sukhoi out to the west following the line of the river.

Gunn checked the Kamov's GPS Satnav which he had programmed with the coordinates which Tanya had given him. He then pressed the 'enter' button a couple of times to bring up the 'distance to destination' information.

'Eighty-four miles to go guys until we reach the location of those coordinates. Could you just pass me my backpack Tanya and I'll programme the coordinates into my Garmin.' Having done that, he looked at the dials in front of him.

'Yea, I was saving that bit of bad news,' Doyle spoke never taking his eyes off the rugged terrain rushing past beneath them. 'We've either used far more fuel because we're flying low and just short of maximum speed or this chopper carries less fuel than I thought or it wasn't filled when we started. You said 84 miles, John. We have enough fuel to get there and to go a few miles further, but certainly not enough to return to Khabarovsk. Can you take control.'

'Sure,' Gunn acknowledged, 'I have control. We should be there in about 12 minutes. I'm going to go back to the east side of the Amur River and hope that we can find an area clear of trees when we decide to land. Gunn glanced at his watch. It was now just before two in the morning. In that Latitude in mid-summer the sun would be appearing over the eastern horizon in the next hour or so. The needle on the dial indicating the weight of fuel on board was now creeping towards the orange sector. The GPS showed forty-one miles to destination.

'The wind's in the north-east so that will help to mask any noise of our approach,' Doyle said, finishing his coffee and sandwich. 'OK, I'll take her, John.'

'You have control,' and Gunn stretched his legs and checked the contents of his pack. The Garmin went into his anorak as did the Glock 17 with a spare magazine. All three of them were quiet as the Kamov's position in Longitude and Latitude on the GPS VDU edged closer to the coordinates which Gunn had programmed into it.

'Ten miles to go. I'm now looking for a place to land,' Doyle muttered as he lowered the Kamovs landing wheels. Below them the the trees of the Taiga offered no gap for an LZ.......eight, seven and then six miles.

'There Doyle! Just to the right. Might just be OK,' Gunn pointed.

'Seen buddy, here goes.' He turned back to the partial clearing and then headed into wind as he held the Kamov in the hover slowly bringing it lower and lower. There was a rush of air as Tanya opened the sliding door, hanging out to give Doyle guidance.

'Ten feet to go!' Tanya shouted. 'Trees very close on both sides.'

'Hold tight guys,' Doyle warned as he brought the Kamov down foot by foot through the gap in the forest canopy. Leaves and twigs, either blown by the downdraft or snapped off by the rotors, flew all round the helicopter. Tanya continued her directions from the open door of the Kamov as it sank lower and lower.

'Wheels are on the ground!' came from Tanya as the helicopter sank into the mossy undergrowth and then all downward motion ceased.

'That's it,' Doyle announced as he shut down the twin turboshaft engines. The rotors came to a halt, leaving only the sound of the cooling engines and the stirring of the taiga's fauna.

CHAPTER 39

Gunn jumped down from the cockpit of the Kamov and pushed his way through the thick undergrowth to the starboard side of the helicopter while Doyle shut down all the instruments. It was still dark so both of them climbed back into the Kamov where they were joined by Doyle who had switched on the lighting in the cabin.

'It'll be light in a couple of hours, so I vote to stay where we are rather than blunder around in the dark,' Doyle suggested.

'There's a little more coffee and a couple of sandwiches which we might as well finish before we resort to any survival measures........if we have a couple of hours I'm going to have a snooze,' and so saying Tanya wrapped her anorak around her, curled up in a corner of the cabin and was soon fast asleep. The chances of anyone finding the Kamov - other than the taiga's fauna - was so remote that both men followed Tanya's example while they waited for it to get light.

All three of them were woken by the sound of scraping on the outside of the sliding door of the Kamov's cabin. It was nearly 7.15 and the sun was shining brightly into the cockpit. Gunn drew the Glock from its shoulder holster and climbed into the cockpit so that he could see who or what was trying to open the door into the Kamov. Outside the helicopter was a very large brown bear rummaging around in the undergrowth outside the helicopter's door. Gunn opened the cockpit door and shouted at the bear.

'What is it?' Doyle asked, leaning into the cockpit.

'It's a bloody great bear who fancies a nibble of us, but fortunately seems far more frightened of us than vice-versa. Come on, it's time we made a move,' and Gunn jumped down from the Kamov, still keeping an eye on the spot where the bear had disappeared into the undergrowth. While Doyle and Tanya sorted out their packs, Gunn switched on his Garmin and programmed in their current position. The Garmin indicated a course of 6° and a distance of 6.5 miles to the coordinates which Tanya had given Gunn. 'Right, let's go,' and Gunn led the way into the forest.

The forest wasn't nearly as dense as they had expected and the conifers were interspersed with deciduous trees such as birch, willow and poplar. The sky was a brilliant blue and the forest was full of wildlife which seemed untroubled by the presence of three humans. But progress was fairly slow and after an hour they had only covered two miles. In another hour they had covered a further two miles. Gunn stopped.

'Can anyone else smell smoke?'

'Sure,' Doyle confirmed quietly.

'Me too,' Tanya agreed.

'OK, let's take it very carefully from here. No idea what the security will involve but there may be movement sensors and trip wires. The abundant wildlife would make those pretty pointless,' Gunn added as an afterthought.

The ground rose steadily over the next mile until it flattened and then dropped away. In the lead, Gunn stopped and dropped to his knees, indicating to the other two to do the same. He then beckoned them both forward.

'Well, there it is........in the exact spot as predicted by those coordinates, Tanya,' and Gunn swung his binoculars across the scene below them. The trees had been thinned on the slope below them and then cleared completely where the gulag had been built. It was identical to the 'Stalag Luft III' he had seen on the film of the 'Great Escape', but it was huge.

The perimeter was surrounded by double fences separated by a gap of 5 metres. There were guard towers every 50 metres and even from where they were they could see the machine guns in the towers. Inside the gulag were rows and rows of wooden huts, each about 50 metres in length. In the centre of all the huts was an open space. Outside the perimeter fences were an assortment of wooden and masonry buildings and a helicopter LZ. It was from one of these buildings that smoke rose from a chimney. All three of them were studying every detail of the gulag.

'How big do you reckon that gulag is?' Gunn whispered.

'At least 500 metres square,' Doyle guessed.

'Just look at the state of the prisoners,' Tanya muttered. 'They look like walking skeletons.'

'And every one of them is Asian, which either supports the KAL flight conspiracy or something quite different. How many were on that flight?' Gunn asked.

'Two or three hundred, but that gulag alone must have more than two or three thousand prisoners. I mean, we can see more than 300 prisoners in the area closest to us,' came from Doyle.

A lorry had just driven into the gulag and six guards jumped down from the back of it. All the guards were Asian. They went into the nearest hut and then in pairs they came out carrying bodies of emaciated prisoners which were thrown into the back of the lorry. Twenty bodies were thrown into the lorry which then drove out of the gulag followed by the six guards who were joking and laughing.

'God help Peter and Ben if that's where they are,' Tanya muttered.

CHAPTER 40

For more than an hour, the three agents watched the gulag through their binoculars.

'Those prisoners are all Asian and look exactly like the living skeletons in the pictures we've all seen of the Nazi concentration camps,' Gunn finally broke the silence.

'All the guards are Asian.......I think Korean. They're certainly not eastern Russian or Mongolian,' Tanya added.

'What the hell is going on down there,' Doyle added. 'There are hundreds....possibly thousands of Japanese, Chinese or Koreans.....men and women in that gulag. I was expecting to find a POW camp with a few hundred prisoners, but this is on an unbelievable scale.'

'I presume that we wait 'til dark before getting any closer?' Tanya asked focusing her binoculars on a pathetically weak prisoner being beaten by a guard.

'Reckon so,' Doyle murmured.

'Did either of you get a chance to do any research on the North Korean gulags?' Tanya asked.

'No, 'fraid not, in my case,' Gunn replied.

'Likewise,' was added by Doyle.

'But I bet you did Tanya,' Gunn teased, 'so come on, bring us up to speed because I have a feeling it's going to prove pretty damn important.'

'OK, while we wait until it gets dark here comes a lesson on the cruellest and most secretive country in the world. If you thought the accounts of the holocaust were appalling, see what you think of this. A conservative estimate......mostly based on satellite photography and reports from those who have escaped from North Korea.....puts the number of gulags at between 30 and 50. All of these are in the northern part of the country, hidden in the deep gorges of the mountainous region. The number of prisoners in these gulags varies from a few thousand to over 50,000 in the case of Gulag 22 - I'll come back to that gulag in a minute. The country has a population of about 24 million. Since internment of suspected dissidents began shortly after the Korean War, the United Nations Commission on Human Rights estimates that some four million prisoners have died in these gulags.... that's about one percent of the population.'

'Do prisoners ever get released from these gulags?' Gunn interrupted.

'Never....the only release from any of these gulags is by death. Where was I?.........oh yes, again, shortly after the Korean War, Kim Il Sung...the Great Leader.....and his Communist government divided the population into three categories. These depended on the role taken by North Koreans in the war, support for the Party, family background and so on. The top grade was the 'elite class' or '*haeksim kyechung*'.....mostly the military....then came 'the wavering class' or '*tonyo kyechung*' and finally 'the hostile class' or '*joktae kyechung*'.'

'The whole country is riddled with spies....people who spy on their neighbours and on everyone and everything. Get this for the epitome of misery, guys. These are just some of the crimes for which not only a family, but the entire extended family can be sent to a gulag.'

'Failing to dust the picture of Kim Jong Il in your house, sitting on a newspaper or magazine that has a picture of the 'Dear leader', being caught trying to forage food for your family from an unofficial source, failing to cheer loud enough at an appearance of the 'Dear Leader', not crying enough at the funeral of a Party official and the list goes on. The most moronically stupid offences will land a family in the gulag....never, ever to reappear except in a cardboard box.'

'Gulag 22?' Doyle queried.

'Ah yes, Gulag 22, which is believed to hold more than 50,000 prisoners. This is the cream on the cake of vile and bestial behaviour. This is the home of the gas chamber and medical experiments on the prisoners. This is where various strains of poisonous gas and other medical experiments have been tested on humans. This is where anyone accused of being in the 'hostile class' is bound to end up. In 2010 North Korea entered a football team for the World Cup in South Africa.'

'Yes, I remember that, but not what happened,' Gunn said.

'The team was drawn against Portugal who thrashed the North Koreans seven/nil. North Korea removed its team from the competition that evening and brought it back to North Korea where all the players, coaches and manager went straight into Gulag 22 without passing 'GO'. They have never been seen again.'

'Kim Jong Il is about to die. He's been ill......sorry for the pun,' Tanya laughed, 'both mentally and physically most of his life. While his people starved and were persecuted he led a life of luxury fed on the best of imported food and provided with as many women as he wanted. No doubt his son Kim Jong Un will take over. He's as barmy as his father and grandfather.'

CHAPTER 41

It was a pleasantly warm day and after Tanya's lesson on the North Korean gulags they took the opportunity to take it in turns to rest before the night's activities. The three of them checked all their equipment before the daylight faded.

'Right guys, the plan of ops for tonight,' Gunn started his briefing. 'First up, Tanya I want you to stay back here as our anchor with the satellite phone........'

'That's fine,' Tanya chipped in, 'I was expecting that and it makes abundant sense, so no argument from me.'

'........good,' Gunn continued. 'I have no idea what to expect when Doyle and I get down there, but I'm clear about our aim on this mission. That is to find and rescue Peter and Ben. Much as I would like to release all those prisoners......if they are Korean........I doubt if they even know that they're in Russia and what the hell would they do if they were set free. I have no idea where this scientist Chong Yejoon might be or even if that information about him is genuine, but if it is true, Tanya, he and any others with him might be wandering around the taiga. We can't use our cellphones any longer so give us 24 hours, Tanya, and then call in the cavalry; questions and suggestions?'

There were none, so Gunn and Doyle slung their small packs on their backs and joined the lengthening shadows in the forest as they moved noiselessly over the spongy moss surface of the Taiga down towards the gulag.

*

'Thompson,' BID's Director reacted to the pulsing light on his phone console.

'Ops Centre sir,' Terry Holt, the Operations Controller, informed his Director. 'London and Langley have both been contacted by the KKS. You might want to see the the demands that have been made.'

'On my way,' and Miles Thompson replaced the phone, left his office telling his PA where he was going and went up the stairs to the 14th floor. He was met by Terry Holt. 'Anything concerning our agents?' he asked.

'Not Gunn, Barnes and Kazakova sir, but it does concern our Ben Warren and the CIA's Peter Samarin.' Terry showed Miles the email that had been sent to the CIA and BID.

From Komitet za Kommercheski Shpionazh - You have arrested two of our agents - Galina Lapayev and Taisia Barkov, known to you as Gilian Lawson and Tricia Baker. I have two of your agents - Benjamin Warren and Peter Samarin. Your agents will be returned to you in exchange for our agents. Signify your agreement to this exchange by publishing this message in the personal columns of the Washington Post and Daily Telegraph - 'Exchange agreed'. If no message within 24 hours your two agents will be executed.

Miles looked at his watch and then asked Terry to contact Gunn on the satellite phone. Tanya Kazakova answered the call.

'Are you able to tell me how long it will take to secure the release of our agents?'

'Twenty-four hours.'

'Thank you,' and Miles nodded to Terry to break the satellite connection.

'Now please connect me to Leon Panetta on the secure line.' The connection was made.

'Yes Miles, do you have any news?

'Hopefully, a result within 24 hours so I'm ready to publish the message if you agree.'

'Thank you for that. We will also publish,' and the connection was broken.

CHAPTER 42

The first part of the downhill approach to the gulag was simple, lit by a bright three-quarter moon, but that soon disappeared behind thick cloud cover leaving the two men in darkness. They both switched on their image intensification night goggles which turned the pitch dark into a clear, eerie green image. Gunn was leading and paused after switching on the II goggles.

'There must be a blackout routine to conceal the location of this camp. I can't see a single light,' he whispered to Doyle.

'Me neither,' Doyle replied, 'but we must now be within a hundred yards of the perimeter fence.'

As predicted by Doyle, the fence loomed out of the night. There wasn't a light or even a chink of a light to be seen anywhere. Gunn turned to the left walking parallel to the fence, but keeping well clear of any trip wires or motion sensitive security devices. Again they both paused.

'They must have a generator to power up this whole camp. I can't believe that this Assassin guy - Zhukov - spends his evenings sitting round a candle or a kerosene lamp,' Doyle whispered.

'Agreed, but in NATO we've had completely silent generators for many years so no reason why the Soviet or Russian Forces shouldn't have them. That looks like the camp's administrative area,' Gunn pointed.

So far they had passed two watch towers, but they were either unmanned at night or the non-smoking discipline was so harsh that not a glowing cigarette tip was visible anywhere. The administrative area was separated from the perimeter fence of the gulag by about 200 yards......'to make sure the stench from the prisoners' latrines didn't upset the guards and administrative staff,' Gunn had commented to Doyle.

The gulag with its wire fence, watch towers and wooden huts appeared to be an exact replica of the German World War Two Stalags, but the buildings of the administrative area were far removed from that construction medium. They had been built out of bricks and mortar or pre-fabricated components for the accommodation blocks and steel-framed hangars and warehouses. In the area which the two agents were approaching they could now identify very small and dim lighting at ground level to provide lit pathways between buildings, but which would be completely invisible above the forest canopy.

They could hear very faint sounds of music, but it seemed that the buildings were not only light blacked-out, but also sound-proofed. A door opened in the building closest to Gunn and Doyle and momentarily the sound of the music increased, but no light showed. Two men had come out of the building. They joined the lit pathway which led towards the gates into the gulag.

'They've got the equivalent of a light-lock rather than an airlock in these buildings,' Doyle whispered when the two men had passed them.

'Any suggestions how we find Ben and Peter,' Gunn asked as they continued their search of the buildings. They had now reached a helicopter LZ with a closed hangar and behind that was what appeared to be an accommodation block which might house at least a couple of hundred guards, Doyle suggested.

'That's diesel exhaust,' Doyle sniffed the air. 'C'mon, let's find this generator and see if we can stir up this place.' They followed their noses until they came to the camp's main generator building. The door was unlocked. They entered the light-lock and as soon as they closed the outer door, the inner door opened into the generator hall. It was a large piece of machinery, made doubly so by all the silenced diesel exhaust trunking and sound insulation - and there were two of them; one in operation and a second as back-up. There were three diesel tanks inside the building, no doubt, Doyle commented, to protect the fuel from the sub-zero winter temperatures. He estimated the tanks contained at least 50,000 gallons each.

At first it seemed that there was no one in the generator building, but the sound of voices - speaking in Russian - alerted the two agents. A stack of heavy wooden packing cases containing machine parts for the generators provided a convenient hiding place. Three men appeared from behind the generators and left the building by the door which Gunn and Doyle had entered.

'I reckon the only way to find Ben and Peter is to stir up this place. Agreed, John?' Doyle asked as he pulled an M84 Stun Grenade out of his back pack and and tucked it into the main power conduits leading out of the generator's switching gear.

'The only other way we're going to find them is to get ourselves captured and that would be pretty pointless. Go for it!'

Doyle pulled the pin out of the grenade and the two men ran out of the building, barely a second before there was a loud explosion and then chaos erupted from every direction.

CHAPTER 43

The blackout routine appeared to have been disrupted by the power cut - such as a broken generator - because emergency lighting came on and lit up both the gulag and the administrative area. Guards poured out of their accommodation building and ran towards the gulag. Gunn and Doyle had removed their goggles. No one took any notice of them. They accepted that this was probably because no one ever came to this remote eastern wilderness of Russia and they were dressed in very similar clothes to the people around them - with the exception of the uniformed guards.

They had moved away from the generator building only seconds before a repair team arrived to inspect the damage. The guards heading for the gulag were all Asian and orders were shouted in Korean. The other inhabitants of the administrative area were Russian.

'The Russians are all heading for that building by the hangar. Let's join them and see if we can find out where our guys are,' Doyle suggested.

'Why not?' and Gunn followed Doyle and all the other men heading towards the hangar. The building was some form of assembly hall or gymnasium and was lit inside by dim emergency lighting. They joined the other people inside. As they entered, instructions were being given by a man standing on a raised platform.

'Is that Zhukov?' Doyle asked.

'No....at least it doesn't look like him.'

Various orders were being issued from the platform and individuals and groups of men responded to these and left the assembly area to carry out the instructions. Doyle gripped Gunn's arm.

'They've just told those two men to go and check on the prisoners.' Doyle's Russian was considerably more fluent than Gunn's. 'C'mon, let's see if the prisoners are our guys.'

They squeezed through the press of men in the assembly area keeping an eye on the two men who left the building just ahead of them. They followed them into a considerably more hospitable part of the gulag which resembled a village of both wooden and brick houses with shops and stores. The two men went to the far end of the village where they stopped by a wooden house. Beyond them was a much larger building.

'Commandant's house?' Gunn whispered.

'Yea, can't see him roughing it with the rest of these people,' Doyle replied.

The two guards entered the wooden building. Gunn and Doyle closed up behind them, both drawing their automatics. The guards were engrossed in the task of checking the locks on the door into the secure area of what appeared to be a 'house arrest' detention building. Together, Gunn and Doyle struck the guards with their automatics and lowered the unconscious men onto the floor. The door into the secure area was locked by bolts on the outside. Once these bolts had been drawn and the door opened, two weary and slightly surprised controllers faced their rescuers.

'Are you guys OK?' Gunn asked.

'Yea, we're OK,' Peter Samarin answered.

'Anything you need from this place?'

'No nothing, except to get the hell out of here!'

'Right, these two can take your place,' and Doyle and Gunn dragged the two guards into what had been Ben and Peter's prison for the last 48 hours.

'No time guys for greetings. Let's get going. Do you know your way around here or have you been in that hut for the last forty-eight hours?' Gunn asked as he led the way back towards the gulag area by a different route.

'We arrived here in the dark and haven't left that hut since they locked us up. Did you guys arrange the power cut?' Ben asked as all four of them jogged between the buildings.

'Doyle fixed the generator,' and even as Gunn spoke, all the emergency lighting went out, leaving only the dim ground level lighting. 'Just in time,' and Gunn and Doyle replaced their image-intensification goggles.

'Do they know you're here?' Peter asked.

'By now they'll know that someone fixed the generator so the answer has to be 'yes',' Doyle answered. 'Is the chopper still here?'

'No, Zhukov told us he was going back to Khabarovsk and then on to Vladivostok to arrange our exchange with some guys in the CIA and BID. I'll explain as much as we know when we get to wherever it is you're taking us,' Peter explained.

'OK, now if you both had our goggles you would be able to see the perimeter fence of the gulag over to our left. We're coming to a long slope up to a crest and then the forest gets much thicker,' Doyle warned the two men.

They were walking in single file with Doyle leading, Peter and Benn behind him and then Gunn bringing up the rear. There was still no sign of pursuit, but Doyle kept up a vigorous pace as he led them through the virgin taiga.

CHAPTER 44

'Ops Centre sir, we've just had a call from John Gunn on the satellite phone.'

'Thanks Terry, and the news?' The BID Director asked glancing at his watch. It was just after 4pm in London so it would be about 2am in Eastern Russian with its 10 hour time difference.

'They've got Ben Warren and the CIA's Peter Samarin. They are now making their way through the forest back to the helicopter which they hi-jacked from the Russian air base in Khabarovsk. There was no mention of the Korean scientist Chong Yejoon. That's it sir.'

'Thank you Terry,' and Miles Thompson replaced the phone. No sooner had he put it down than it rang again.

'Personal call for you, sir, from Leon Panetta,' his PA told him before connecting him to the Head of the CIA.

'Our boys have done us well, Miles. No mention of this Korean scientist, Chong, but I think we all guessed that might be a ruse to keep our interest before the exchange of agents was demanded.'

'Agreed Leon, I expect we'll get a lot more information when they've had a chance to debrief your Peter Samarin and our Ben Warren. In the interim, let's hope they get clear of the taiga and any pursuit by Zhukov and his goons.'

'OK, well let's wait and see what his next communication says now that he's lost his bargaining chips,' Panetta suggested.

'Agreed, I don't think we'll have long to wait,' and the Director of BID ended the call.

*

After meeting up with Tanya and making the satellite call to the CIA and BID, the five-strong group pressed on through the forest as dawn broke behind them. It was nearly 6am by the time the Garmin GPS led them back to the Kamov helicopter.

'How are you guys feeling?' Gunn asked the two controllers who were looking exhausted after struggling through the thick undergrowth for the last four hours.

'Pretty knackered,' Ben was the first to reply. 'Look, we've got lots to pass on as Zhukov insisted on bragging about his KKS organistaion, but I expect the most urgent thing we need to do is get out of here. How much fuel have you got?'

Doyle was already in the cockpit going through the start-up procedure for the Kamov's two turboshaft engines.

'Something between 50 and 100 miles max,' he announced.

'Yes, I thought that might be the case. Have you got your maps?' Ben asked. Gunn opened his backpack and removed the silk-printed map of Eastern Russia from Latitude 40° to 60° North and Longitude 100° to 140° East, covering the entire Khabarovsk region. 'Ah, thanks,' and Ben studied it for a moment. 'About 50 miles north of us there's a branch line of the Baikal-Amur Mainline railway which runs west from the port of Vanino on the east coast to where it links with the main BAM line at Komsomolsk. About 40 miles before that junction is a station....here, it's marked on this map....Selikhino. That station is just over 50 miles from here.

If we could make it there we could get the train which goes all the way to Moscow.'

'Sounds like a good plan to me,' Doyle said from the cockpit. 'Climb aboard everyone and if you could sing out the coordinates of that station, John, I'll feed it into the Kamov's GPS and we can get this bird back in the sky.'

Tanya and Gunn helped the other two into the Kamov. Gunn went forward to the co-pilot's seat and Tanya took up her position by the door to guide Doyle out of the forest. As soon as Tanya told Doyle that they were all buckled up in the cabin, he started the engines, shattering the early morning stillness of the taiga.

CHAPTER 45

'Hang on Tanya!' Doyle's warning was addressed to her as she was the only one in the Kamov's cabin with a headset plugged into the intercom circuit. 'The undercarriage has sunk into the deck so we'll come clear with a jolt.......strapped in?'

'I'm strapped in....go for it Doyle!' Tanya encouraged, hanging on tightly to the handrail by the open door.

Doyle increased the power and applied maximum lift to the collective pitch. The Kamov shuddered with the effort of extracting its wheels from the spongy undergrowth and then, exactly as warned by Doyle, shot skywards like an express lift. Leaves, small branches and debris swirled all round the helicopter as Doyle struggled to steady it. How the rotors either missed all the larger trees, which would have certainly destroyed the steel and carbon-fibre blades, or survived the smaller branches was a mystery to Tanya, but the helicopter rose clear of the taiga and then headed north-east towards the rising sun.

'We always joked that the Ruskies built their planes like brick shit-houses, and now I believe it,' Doyle commented on the Kamov's lift-off from the taiga. 'OK John, what's the GPS tells us?'

'Course is 352° and distance to the station on the BAM railway is 110 kilometres,' Gunn replied.

'Got that, and how are our two guys back with you Tanya?'

'Both fast asleep and undisturbed by your exhibition of flying skill. I'll leave them be and we can hear their account of what happened to them later,' Tanya answered.

'Makes sense, now let's see if I can coax a few extra miles out of this chopper. Christ! I'd give a year's pay for a hot coffee and bagel.'

'What are the chances of a fast-food stall at that station?' Tanya fantasised.

'Less than zero, but dreaming about it might pass the time,' Gunn answered.

'I know this'll use up more fuel, but I'm gonna take this chopper in a wide circuit out to the west. Back at the gulag, they'll know the generator was blown and they might have discovered the loss of their two bargaining chips, but they must be wondering how it all happened. That's my assessment anyway and I don't intend to give them any clues. With a bit of luck they don't even know that we got here in a chopper. Even if they sussed that out they won't know which way we've gone,' which was how Doyle explained his deviation out to the west to his crew.

Having made the detour out to the west, staying well clear of sight or sound of anyone at the gulag, the GPS then gave Doyle a new course to the the station on the BAM railway. The distance was now 85 kilometres....a shade over 50 miles. The Kamov was flying at just over 100mph - its most beneficial endurance cruising speed, but the fuel gauges for the two Rybinsk engines were both in the orange sectors and close to moving into the red. The Kamov had no reserve fuel tanks. The helicopter was flying at no more than tree-top height with the sole intention of staying clear of any air-defence radars - notorious in this part of Russia since the KAL 747 incident in 1983.

'What do you reckon, John,' Doyle broke a period of silence as both men had their eyes riveted on the fuel gauges.

'Climb to 1,000 feet to give us airspace to auto-rotate if we run out of gas and risk being picked up on the air-defence radars or stay low and cross our fingers?'

Gunn pressed the mode button on the GPS which altered the information displayed from 'course' to 'distance to next waypoint'. It showed 18 miles. The needles on both fuel gauges were in the red sector....no reserve. Even as he glanced at them the audible warning was triggered.

'Hell, my fingers are crossed already so let's stay low and make it as difficult as possible for the radars.'

'Roger to that....I make it just seven minutes. Can you see what looks like a track through the forest below us?'

'Spotted that a couple of minutes ago and there seem to be small clearings on either side every half mile or so....like passing places. They look large enough to take this machine.'

'Again....roger to that....I'm taking her down. Can you wake up our crew and get them ready for what might be a bumpy landing.'

'Will do,' and Gunn checked with Tanya who confirmed that all three of them were awake and ready for the landing.

CHAPTER 46

The low-fuel warning alarm changed from intermittent bleeps to a strident, continuous shriek as Doyle brought the Kamov into the hover above the track through the forest. Juggling the use of the collective stick throttle on his left side and using a combination of the cyclic stick between his knees and the foot pedals controlling the pitch of the tail rotor, he side-slipped the helicopter over the centre of a cleared passing-area on the right side of the track. Throughout this manoeuvre Tanya provided Doyle with a constant feed-back of directions to keep the rotors clear of the trees.

'All clear!....take her down,' Tanya urged Doyle as the first engine splutter told them there wasn't even fuel vapour left in the tanks. Doyle lowered the collective stick and the Kamov sank down into the taiga once more as the two Rybinsk engines spluttered, coughed and then shut down.

'It's 'shanks pony' from here guys,' Gunn announced, climbing out of the co-pilot's seat into the back of the Kamov. Tanya already had the door open and the four of them climbed down on to the ground. 'This track has been used quite recently,' Gunn remarked as he studied the wheel tracks of a heavy vehicle. 'Let's get going before we get proof of what made those tracks. It should be no more than five or six miles to the rail track.'

The five of them set off along the track, but had only been walking for about twenty minutes when Gunn, who was leading, stopped.

'Vehicle coming!....quick guys, into the forest,' and he led them off the track to the right where they were completely concealed by the thick undergrowth. The noise of a large vehicle or vehicles grew louder and louder until a khaki-painted military truck appeared over a crest in the track some 200 yards ahead of them. The first vehicle was followed by seven more. Gunn turned to Ben Warren who was crouched beside him.

'Any idea what this lot might be?'

'Possibly......I'll explain more fully later,' Ben replied, 'but if there're Koreans in the back of these trucks then Peter and I know exactly what's going on. Zhukov took great delight in telling us of all his thoroughly evil and profitable entrepreneurial ventures of which this is but one.'

As the trucks went past them Ben's prediction was proved right. The trucks were fitted out as troop carriers. At the rear of each truck were two armed Russians guarding a truck full of ethnic Asians. The last truck to pass them was full of Asian women and children.

'C'mon on.....I'll explain later what this is all about,' Ben offered, 'but it won't be long before the discovery of the helicopter is reported back to the gulag. If Zhukov has returned with his helicopter then he will be up here in no time.'

No further encouragement was needed and the five of them set off at a brisk pace for the last couple of miles to the BAM station at Selikhino. After half-an-hour, they saw isolated signs of civilisation - wooden houses and sheds, farm animals and.....people. Apart from the occasional show of interest in them, their progress was ignored. The single line rail track ran along the southern side of the town of Selikhino and then just before the station itself there was a marshalling yard of half a dozen tracks on one of which were two huge steam engines.....'nirvana for any train-spotting anoraks' Ben had remarked.......connected to some fifty or more wagons of all shapes and purposes. Ben pointed at the cattle trucks. 'That's what those unfortunate Koreans would have travelled in.' No one replied. The similarity to the horrors of the Holocaust, the rail sidings in Belsen and the Nazi concentration camps was only too vivid.

When they reached the rail track Gunn stopped. They could see the station about 200 yards away to their left. 'I'd like to wait here for a while in spite of the fact that Zhukov might not be far behind us. With the frequent use of these sidings for the cattle trucks that carry these North Koreans, Zhukov must have contacts in this town, particularly contacts to do with the station. Make sense?' Gunn queried. There were murmurs of agreement. 'If we all rush into the station and buy tickets to Moscow, how long do you think it will be before Zhukov knows where we're headed?' Again there were murmurs of agreement. 'Tanya, I would like you to do a recce for us. Russian is your native language and Zhukov can't as yet know that you are with us. I would like you to find out the train timings, not only to Moscow, but also to the east coast. We will wait here.'

'Will do,' and Tanya left her backpack with the four men and headed for the station.

While they waited for her to return, it gave Ben and Peter a chance to explain to the other three what they had discovered from Zhukov.

CHAPTER 47

'What did you guys learn from Zhukov,' Doyle asked the two controllers.

'You want to kick off, Peter?' Ben offered.

'Sure, so let's start with Zhukov......the self-styled 'Assassin'. He obviously has no one else to boast about his entrepreneurial success and so was really keen to brag to us about selling sensitive Western intel to the World's pariah states. Both Ben and I realised that this looked pretty grim for our chances of survival having given us all this information. We reckoned that Zhukov had no intention of exchanging us for those two women.'

'He learned well under his KGB master, Volkonoff. Even before Volkonoff was killed, the two of them had been making use of their KGB skills, training and contacts to set up the Komitet za Kommercheskii Schpionazh',' he paused. 'You both know.......' but nods indicated that he should continue. 'This was a scheme to make money - lots of it. It had nothing to do with safeguarding the 'Motherland' from the West's intelligence agents and spies. The plan was to get moles and sleepers into key positions in the West's intelligence organisations and then sell the information this produced to a waiting list of clients of which there was no shortage......North Korea, Iraq, Iran, Burma, Yemen, Libya, Syria, to name but a few of the World's pariah states. They also planted sleepers in Western cities to act as messengers or go-betweens to get the information back to Moscow. Ben, why don't you take over from here.'

'OK, so Faraway Travel was set up with agencies in most of the Western capitals, but its main training centre was in Manchester. Every year these sleepers or messengers would go on a package tour to Russia during which they would pass on specific intelligence or just general items, particularly any material which could be used to blackmail Western politicians and business magnates. We now know how successful this was, having identified BID's and the CIA's moles. Zhukov gives himself the title of 'Assassin', a title he well deserves, but it was Anatoli Vadin who was sent to England to kill the three genuine tourists on that package holiday to Russia. It was Zhukov and his psychopathic lust for brutality who slaughtered those sleepers when he realised that both the CIA and BID were closing in on his agents and KKS operation. So, back to you Peter to deal with the CD that was planted amongst Mrs Hurst's CD collection by Zhukov after he had tortured and then killed her.'

'Sure....' Peter continued, 'when the Indianapolis Police found her she had been tortured, mutilated and then decapitated. Zhukov told us that Mrs Hurst finally confessed to being less than discreet about her role which is probably how our section in Langley picked up on Merton and the existence of another double agent in the CIA. Zhukov had no idea what she might have said to the other sleepers on that package tour from England, Sweden and Belgium. So he decided to kill all of them. That was a true indication of Zhukov's bestiality. So what's with the saga of KAL Flight 007 and the scientist Chong Yejoon? Zhukov boasted to us that he was particularly pleased with this little ruse. There was a South Korean scientist named Chong Yejoon on that flight which the Soviets shot down. The conspiracy theories surrounding what happened to the passengers, if all or any survived the crash, may or may not be true. One thing we are sure about is that none of them are in the gulag where we were locked up.'

'So what the hell are all those Koreans doing in the Gulag?' Gunn asked.

'Just another money making operation set up between Zhukov and Kim Jong Il,' Peter continued. 'Tanya told me on the walk here that she had briefed you on the North Korean gulags. Nothing has changed for years. Back in 1940 the Russians used the port of Vanino on the east coast to transport dissidents and convicts to Magadan and from there to the Kolyma gulag labour camps. Zhukov, during a trip to North Korea, offered to take the pressure off the North Koreans, who were running out of resources to build gulags, by shipping their unwanted dissidents to gulags in Russia....at a price of course. Whether Putin and the Russian Government were either aware of or complicit in this deal we have no idea, but judging by the level of corruption in Russia nothing would surprise me.'

'So these wretched people, who have done nothing worse than forget to polish a picture of the 'Dear Leader', are taken by cattle truck to Najin - a port on the north-east coast of North Korea where they are loaded into a cargo ship which then takes three days to cover the 1,000 miles to Vanino on the east coast of Russia. They aren't fed, watered or provided with any toilet facilities during this voyage. On arrival they are all hosed down to clean them up and loaded into the cattle trucks you can see over there in the marshalling yard. On arrival here they are loaded into the trucks which you saw and taken to the gulag where they get their first meal in four days. Needless to say by the time they reach the gulag the number has decreased by a factor of a third.'

'Jeezus!' Doyle muttered. 'And this character Chong?'

'Oh that was just a ploy to get the CIA and BID to send two of their agents to investigate. The two agents would be taken hostage and offered in exchange for the return of their two top agents, Taisia Barkov in London and Galina Lapayev in Langley.'

'But they got you two instead,' Doyle finished.

'Yea.'

'So what was the purpose of the assassination attempt at Khabarovsk Station?' Gunn asked.

'I'll pass that to you Ben.'

'We only learned about that from you after our rescue, but Peter and I discussed an explanation before we fell asleep in the back of the helicopter. The only explanation we can come up with is that Zhukov did not believe that Tanya was working for the KKS. Whatever he may be, he's no fool and I suspect that he had decided to eliminate any uncertainty by giving Georgy Balashov the task of killing her.

'But if Balashov hadn't taken a shot at Tanya, what would we have discovered about this supposed South Korean, Chong?' Doyle asked.

'Just a guess, but having identified herself to the girl at the BAM information desk, she would have either told Tanya the location of the house in Malinkovskaya Street or handed her a card with the address. So any agents sent by BID or the CIA would have gone to number 57, been taken hostage and flown up to the gulag,' Ben suggested.

'What about those four guys who Tanya met up with at the house in Khabarovsk........Ilya, Alexei, Slava and Irena,' Doyle asked. 'Where had they come from?'

'Certainly not from that Korean Airlines flight; they were too young. They're all in their early twenties. It's now thirty years since that plane was shot down. I think they had been brought up in the village that developed around the gulag and knew no other life than doing as they were told by Zhukov.'

CHAPTER 48

Tanya returned from her recce of the station carrying three large paper bags.

'Here you are guys. All stations on the BAM and Trans Siberian Railways have food and hot drink stalls on the platforms. Sorry, no hot tea as I couldn't carry four paper cups, but there should be enough in those bags to stave off your hunger.'

The four men fell on the iced buns and cakes.

'The first train heading west towards Tynda isn't due for another forty-five minutes and crosses at this station.....so I was told by the ticket clerk.....with the east-bound train to Sovetskaya Gavan. They will both be in the station for about five minutes. Russian trains are always on time so we need to get a move on with our plans.'

'OK, let's look at the map,' Gunn said finishing off a sickly sweet iced bun. Doyle produced the map which they spread out on the grass below the rail embankment. Tanya produced the timetable which she had been given at the station.

'The west-bound BAM goes to Komsomolsk and on to Tynda, then north of Lake Baikal and finally on to Moscow via Bratsk, Novosibirsk, Omsk and Yekaterinburg. The east-bound train goes to Sovetskaya Gavan via Vysokogorniy and the port of Vanino. Tynda is about 500 miles away. The BAM gets there at 0300 hours tomorrow. Sovetskaya Gavan is about 200 miles away and the BAM will get there at 2130 hours tonight,' Tanya paused while Gunn and Doyle studied the map.

'OK, so let's take the worst case scenario from our point of view,' Gunn continued, turning to Ben. 'You said that Zhukov had gone to Vladivostok. Was that in his helicopter?'

'Only as far as Novy Airport in Khabarovsk. He told us he would then change to his own private plane....he enjoyed boasting about that.....I think he told us that it was a Gulfstream...for the 600 mile flight to Vladivostok.'

'Right.....so the convoy of trucks would have seen our helicopter, but would have been unaware of the power-cut and your escape until they reached the gulag......say, about two hours later. Agreed?'

'Yea, I reckon that's about right so that would have been about 8 or 9 this morning,' from Doyle.

'Let's say 8....remember worst case,' Gunn continued. 'The gulag then contacts Zhukov; we know they can communicate because we saw the aerials. He gets in his private plane and flies to Khabarovsk, picks up his helicopter.......any recollection of the size of his helicopter Ben....Peter?' Gunn interrupted his chain of thought.

'Exactly the same as the one you hi-jacked from the airbase. Why?' Ben asked.

'The Kamov can carry 16 fully armed soldiers in addition to its flight crew,' Doyle supplied the information. 'In the worst case scenario, that tells us the size of the opposition we could be up against.'

'So Zhukov gets the bad news at 8. Let's say he's airborne in his plane by 9. An hour and a half to Novy Airport, he then changes to his helicopter followed by an hour's flight to the gulag where he arrives by mid-day....give or take twenty minutes. So he gets to the gulag at about the same time as the trains leave Selikhino?' Gunn ended with a note of query to see if there was agreement. Doyle had been studying the silk-printed map.

'Yea.....agreed,' Doyle said looking up from the map, 'but that's worst case. I think we might allow ourselves a little bit of slack in those timings. But here's something else. Let's say Zhukov and his gooks get in the helicopter and set off to catch the train. That Kamov of his has a max range of 400 miles and no reserve. It's at least 600 miles to Tynda from the gulag so he doesn't have the range to get there before us, unless he has a fuel dump somewhere. That means he will have to stop this train before it gets to Tynda.' There was silence for a moment and then Tanya upset all their calculations.

'What if Zhukov were to fly his Gulfstream direct to Tynda. He would be landing there just about now, giving him ample time to prepare a reception for our arrival.'

'Ben, can you and Peter have a look at this map with Tanya while Doyle and I get in touch with BID and the CIA to give them a sitrep,' and Gunn moved away from the map.

It was the night duty officer in the Communications Centre who took Gunn's secure call to BID.

'We're in a town called Selikhino in eastern Russia and about to board the BAM train either westwards to Moscow or eastwards to Sovetskaya Gavan. Our first stop west would be Tynda about 500 miles to the west where we are due to arrive at 0320 hours tomorrow. If we go east we reach Sovetskaya Gavan on the east coast at 2130 hours tonight. It's likely that Zhukov will do everything he can to prevent us getting away with his hostages. While on the train you will only be able to contact us on this secure phone by text. Barnes will be sending the same information to Langley. In order to make a decision we need to know from you in the next ten minutes if there are airports at Tynda and Sovetskaya Gavan and your recommendation whether we go east or west.' As soon as Gunn had sent his message, Doyle contacted the CIA Headquarters in Langley.

CHAPTER 49

It was only just a shade over five minutes before the satellite phone buzzed. The call was from Langley.

'Both Tynda and Sovetskaya Gavan have useable airports. Sigikta Airport is ten miles to the north of Tynda and has one main runway. Yuzhno-Sakhalinsk Airport is on the northern outskirts of Sovetskaya Gavan and also has one runway. Both airports can handle multi-engine jet aircraft. On balance, our recommendation is to go for the east coast. Let us know your decision and we will make plans to assist. London agrees this recommendation.'

'May I make a suggestion,' Ben offered.

'Of course,' the others encouraged.

'If we all go into the station and buy five tickets to Tynda or Sovetskaya, how long will it be before that information gets back to Zhukov? Not long I suggest. The advice from London and Langley is to go to Sovetskaya Gavan. I think that makes sense as it's less fraught with problems extracting us from the east coast than from somewhere between here and Tynda....or Moscow......any violent disagreement so far?'

Heads were shaken.

'Right then; why don't we all go into the station and buy tickets to Moscow....or Tynda, ensuring that the ticket clerk or whoever takes note of us. Tanya has told us that the west-going train gets in first followed by the east-going one. She says they are both in the station for about five minutes. My plan is that we board the west-going train to Tynda and when the other train stops beside it, we climb down from one train and up into the other out of sight of the ticket office. Sure, we will have no valid tickets for the journey to Sovetskaya Gavan, but I'm sure we can talk or buy our way out of that problem.'

'What do we do if the east train is late?' Doyle asked.

'We go as far as the first stop.....that would be Komsomolsk, and then catch the next east-going train.' Ben looked round at the four of them. He was just about to ask for suggestions when the satellite phone buzzed.

'Take the east-bound train to Sovetskaya Gavan but leave it at the Port of Vanino. The container port is on the south side of the Tumnin River estuary. There is a South Korean container ship now loading at berth Number 4 of that container terminal. It will sail at 2330 hours (East Russia local time) tonight. The ship's name is 'Unsongja' which is 'Transporter' in English. The Captain of the ship will give you new instructions when you board.'

'We've got twenty-five minutes until the Tynda train arrives,' Gunn announced looking at his watch. 'I'm in favour of Ben's plan. Anyone not in favour?'

There were no dissenters, so the five set off for the station which they reached five minutes later. They went into the ticket office in the entrance hall of the station and made quite sure that the clerk and the station manager knew that four of them intended to go to Tynda. They had agreed that Tanya would remain apart from the four men and buy her ticket separately.

The controllers had readily agreed that the two intelligence organisations could afford to buy five first class tickets Tynda. This would be remembered by the ticket clerk as only tourists could afford to buy such expensive tickets. Their two-berth first class compartments were in the 'spalny vagon. Second class had four berth compartments in a 'kupe' carriage and third class - 'platskartny' - had bunks in an open-plan dormitory carriage.

Once the tickets had been bought, they went out onto the boarding area and bought hot cups of tea from the samovars on the food barrows while they waited for the west-bound train. Proving Tanya's statement true about punctuality, a series of loud whistle blasts announced the arrival of the smart blue and red diesel-electric BAM train which would eventually complete its journey in Moscow in six days time. The train stopped and steps were positioned to help the passengers climb down from the coaches.

Gunn and Doyle tried to avoid constant glances to the west in the hope of seeing the arrival of the train to the east coast. There was a blast from the train's whistle.

'That's just the warning whistle,' Tanya reassured them.

As the echo of the whistle faded it was taken up by three sharp blasts from the east-bound BAM which appeared round a bend in the track. The five agents boarded the second coach behind the restaurant car of the west-bound train. The other train came to a halt alongside them and its passengers climbed down to the ground-level boarding area to leave the train or buy food and hot or cold drinks.

There were three loud whistle blasts from their train. 'Time to go guys,' and Gunn led the way, climbing down from the train and up the steps of the train on the other track. Tanya was the last to climb up to the east-bound train. As she closed the door behind her, the west-bound train pulled out of the station.

No one on the train had seen their arrival as the majority of the passengers had alighted to buy food and drinks.

CHAPTER 50

After three loud whistle blasts which sent passengers hurrying along the platform to re-board the train, the east-bound BAM pulled slowly out of the station. The agents made their way forward from the third class compartment which they had boarded from the west-bound train. In front of the first class compartment was the restaurant car and bar which is where they met up with a buxom woman whose uniform identified her as the train's ticket inspector.

They all produced their tickets and after the furore of explaining that they were on the right train, but had bought the wrong tickets - and a generous tip - she endorsed all their tickets with first class compartment numbers.

Within ten miles of leaving the station, the BAM began its winding route along a gorge through the Sikholte-Alin range of hills. The taiga scenery and the wild life all round the track would have been a tourist sight to enjoy had it not been contaminated by the horror of the men, women and children, herded like cattle into trucks, who had so recently travelled along the track to suffer a lifetime of hard labour, starvation and brutality in a gulag.

With only the occasional diversion, the track hugged the southern banks of various tributaries leading west to the Amur River and then the climb began to the highest point in the route to the coast at the town of Vysokogorniy. There, the track joined the east-flowing Tumnin River valley in the shadow of the 5,000 foot mountain, Gora Komandnaya. All five of the agents couldn't believe that their luck in escaping from Zhukov could hold much longer. But at 1650 hours to the minute of the scheduled arrival time, the BAM pulled into the station at Vysokogorniy without any attempt by Zhukov to impede their escape to the port of Vanino.

The satellite phone buzzed. Tanya pressed the receive button to accept a secure text from Langley.

'Signal traffic in your sector of Eastern Russia has increased significantly in the last four hours. Orbit of KH-12 has been adjusted to overfly your sector. This has revealed an increase in air traffic in the coastal region of Vanino and Sovetskaya Gavan.'

'Hardly surprising,' Tanya commented as she showed the text to the others.

'No, but I would have put my money on an interception of this train in some remote part of its route to the coast. I still can't decide whether Zhukov is running this KKS spy network as a private enterprise or whether he has the support - whether overt or tacit - of the FSB,' Ben muttered as he read the text.

The train pulled out of the station and continued to climb slowly to the highest point on the route to the coast. An additional engine had been added at Vysokogorniy to help the train up the incline. In order to reach the summit, the track ran along the south bank of the fast flowing Tumnin River through a steep-sided gorge. The train was crawling along at little more than a brisk walking pace.

'It's bloody frustrating not being able to see ahead,' Gunn said as he stared out of the window and then went to the end of the coach and tried the door. It wasn't locked and swung open inwards. By standing on the boarding step and holding onto the handrail on either side of the door he was able to get a good view of the track ahead. The train was going round a long left-hand bend which gave Gunn a good view of what lay ahead of the BAM.

'Bugger!'

'Problem buddy?' Doyle asked who was standing just inside the doorway.

'Yea, there's a rock-fall across the track about 500 yards ahead of the train. Ah! you've got your binos. Can you check the rock-fall.'

'Sure.' Doyle focused his binoculars on the rock face above the rock-fall as the train came to a halt. 'There's nothing natural about that fall. Hard to see without binos, but there's a char mark on the rock face left by the explosive used to bring down the rocks across the track. I can't see anyone in the area of the rock-fall..........'

'No, that's because they're behind us,' came from Tanya who was in the doorway on the other side of the coach.

'OK, time to get moving. Grab your packs and let's get out of here,' Gunn stepped back from the doorway and went to the door on the other side from where Tanya had spotted the men approaching the train. Ben and Peter were waiting in the corridor holding Doyle's and Gunn's packs.

'I think the only way to avoid this lot is to climb up the side of the gorge.......they're now all boarding the train two coaches down from us. We're fresh out of time guys,' Tanya warned them.

'Right...Tanya you lead the way and find a route up the side of the gorge. Ben....Peter, you follow Tanya and Doyle and I'll bring up the rear,' and Gunn then followed Doyle off the train onto the gravel of the track ballast.

The rock face of the gorge on the side away from the river was considerably steeper than the one on the other side of the river as it had been blasted by explosive to take the BAM track. Tanya had seen that the two controllers were wearing leather-soled shoes which were highly unsuitable for any form of rock climbing. She and the other agents were all wearing trainers - not much better. She spotted a natural fissure in the rock face which might make the climb less hazardous and also provide some concealment - for a short while - from the men searching the train. She turned to Ben.

'I think you've done some climbing?'

'A little, in the Peak District.'

'OK, you go first. I think this is what professional climbers call a chimney. Tuck right into the side of it.'

'Got that,' and Ben wasted no time finding foot and hand holds as he started to climb.

'Peter, what about you?'

'Yea, I've done a bit. Catch me if I fall will you!' and with that request he followed Ben. Tanya followed the two men, urging them on and guiding them to foot and hand holds. The chimney gave Gunn and Doyle good concealment from the people on the train, but as they moved forward with their search that concealment would be lost.

Ben was climbing well and just over half way up the side of the gorge. Peter was some ten feet behind him and Tanya was just a few feet behind Peter. Gunn and Doyle had yet to start climbing.

There was a shout from the train followed by a shot. The bullet ricocheted off the rock face level with Ben and then to Gunn's horror Ben almost fell back off the face, but just managed to save himself. Even from where Gunn was he could see the blood on Ben's left arm.

CHAPTER 51

There were five of them. All dressed in Russian Army combat clothing. There may have been more on the train, but the quick glance that Gunn had taken round the edge of the fissure had resulted in a volley of automatic fire which gouged chunks of rock off the edge of the rock face where his head had been.

'They're off the train and on this side of it. Can you give me a 'Willie Pete' from your pack.'

'Sure,' and Doyle removed an M15 white phosphorous smoke grenade - known in the US Army as a Willie Pete - from his pack and handed it to Gunn. The 'soldiers' were now only some twenty yards away.

'What's the fuze on these?' Gunn asked, squeezing the detonator release lever and removing the pin.

'Four seconds.'

'Got it,' and Gunn released the lever, counted two and hurled the grenade round the edge of the fissure at the group of soldiers. The grenade exploded while still in the air showering the men with white hot globules of phosphorous causing the most horrific burns - right down to the bone - to any exposed skin. Both Gunn and Doyle rolled clear of the fissure and using their automatics shot all five men. The wind funnelling along the gorge carried the smoke back along the train. There was no visible movement anywhere else, but at the head of the train the drivers had walked forward to inspect the rock-fall. The moment the shooting started all four men from the two engines had vanished.

'C'mon, let's go,' and Doyle started the climb up the fissure with Gunn close behind him. Above them, Tanya had climbed past Peter and was now beside Ben, helping him up the last twenty feet of the rock face by placing his one good hand in handholds. As soon as Tanya and Ben reached the top of the gorge, she removed her pack and broke open her first aid kit. The ricochet had not lodged in Ben's arm, but had made a deep flesh wound which made his left arm unusable. Gasping for breath, Peter joined them at the top of the gorge followed by Doyle and Gunn.

Below them, the smoke from the white phosphorous grenade had cleared and nervous passengers had dismounted from the train and were examining the five soldiers by the side of the track. One or two pointed to the top of the gorge. Gunn went over to Ben. Tanya had just injected a syrette of morphine into the muscle on Ben's other arm.

'How're you feeling?' Gunn asked.

'Not so bad....perhaps a bit light-headed as the morphine takes affect....both legs and my other arm are fine so I'm ready to move whenever you say so. What's the plan?' Ben asked.

'Hey, I'd love to pretend I have a plan, but any further than getting away from Zhukov's men hasn't currently reached the planning stage.'

'If those five guys down there were sent to stop the train and kill or capture us they must have got here by chopper,' Doyle concluded and then continued, 'there's no other form of transport that could have got them here ahead of the train. Somewhere ahead of this train.....possibly where the track bends round the gorge to the right after this left-hand bend.....there should be a chopper. Here's my suggestion guys. Tanya stays here with Peter and Ben and I go on a recce with John to find the chopper.'

'Makes sense, but I suggest that we all move away from this exposed position into the forest where there's better concealment,' Tanya said, getting to her feet. All five of them followed her lead and the rocky ground of the gorge soon gave way to the moss and lichen-covered ground of the forest.

'Was Zhukov amongst those guys down there?' Doyle asked as they reached the cover of the trees and undergrowth.

'No idea,' Gunn replied. 'I've never seen him. What does he look like?' Gunn addressed his query to Tanya, Ben and Peter.

'You can't miss him.....he's an ugly bastard with a shaved head and pierced ears,' Peter offered and then added, 'coming to think of it, these days, that could fit quite a few people.'

'None of the guys we shot was wearing any head dress and none had a shaved head so we might find him at the chopper.....if there is a chopper. C'mon John, let's see if we can find the bastard,' and the two men set off through the forest.

The route Doyle chose was along the edge of the forest where they were able to make quicker progress. As predicted by Doyle, the gorge curved round to the right following the course of the river, revealing a part of the track that was out of sight of the rock-fall across the rails. They both dropped to a crouch as they approached the edge of the gorge. For the last few yards they crawled forward on their stomachs. Below them the base of the gorge opened out for about 200 yards before it narrowed once again. In the middle of the open space by the river was a Kamov helicopter with four men visible - two of them wearing flying overalls.

'Probably used as a maintenance area when the track was being built,' Doyle suggested, removing the binoculars from his pack.

'No sign of the shaven-headed Zhukov,' Gunn commented as he also studied the scene below them to identify a possible approach to the group by the helicopter.

'They'll be expecting their guys to return from the direction of the sabotaged track so if we can find any form of cover to get close from the other direction, that'd be good. Whatever we do we need to do it quickly before they get curious and do a recce of the train. There might have been more of Zhukov's guys on the train,' Doyle added.

'Sure......let's find a way down to the track,' Gunn agreed as the two men crawled away from the gorge edge and then started looking for an easy way down from the top of the gorge which Ben would be able to manage.

CHAPTER 52

It took no more than a few minutes for Gunn and Doyle to find a route down from the top of the gorge to the rail track below.....'probably an animal track to get to the river,' Gunn had remarked, as they scrambled down the steep path.

'Ben should manage this alright, but if we get hold of that chopper could you hold it in the hover with one side of the landing gear on the top of the gorge? There would be no need to waste time going back to collect Ben, Tanya and Peter,' Gunn suggested.

'I'd been thinking about that. A lot depends on how much fuel is left. Holding a chopper in a static hover uses up pounds of fuel in no time as you will know only too well.'

They had reached the track and were able to stay out of sight of the helicopter and its crew as long as they stayed close to the rock face of the gorge, but as soon as they moved they would be in full view until they reached the river bank. This meant that they had to cross the track and open ground for about seventy yards with no cover to hide from the crew. Gunn dropped to a crouch and peered round the jumble of boulders at the foot of the rock face.

'Can't see the chopper pilots....I think they're back inside the Kamov. The other two are walking in the direction of the train. Ready?'

'Yea, ready.'

'OK!' and Gunn set off across the open ground, expecting any second to hear the crack of a shot or a shout from the direction of the helicopter. He jumped over the side of the river bank and slid down the gravel and shale to the edge of the fast flowing water. Doyle tumbled down the bank to join him.

'Think we made it?' Doyle gasped catching his breath.

'No sign that we've been seen,' Gunn said peering over the side of the river bank. 'Hey, look what was out of sight on the other side of the chopper.'

'What's that?' Doyle asked as he crawled up the river bank to join Gunn.

'Four, forty gallon drums of fuel with a hand-cranked transfer pump. That's why there were so few of Zhukov's men on the Kamov. They were carrying their own fuel supply.'

'That's a real bonus. Ready when you are. Same routine as we did in the multi-storey car park?'

'OK, you take left and I'll take right. Go!' and both men covered the distance to the Kamov without alerting the two crewmen who were almost out of sight round the bend in the gorge or the pilots in the helicopter. The sliding side door of the passenger compartment was open and contained no nasty surprises. The car park routine worked again and the unconscious pilots were laid out on the ground by the empty fuel drums. Doyle came round and climbed into the right-hand pilot's seat while Gunn climbed into the back of the Kamov. There was nothing in the passenger cabin except two Kalashnikov assault rifles.

'Hey, John, we've got a full fuel load,' Doyle exclaimed from the front as he switched on the instruments. 'OK, here we go,' and he powered up the twin turbo-shaft engines. Both crewmen had disappeared round the blind bend in the gorge some 200 yards away, but within seconds of the engine starting they reappeared. Gunn climbed into the passenger compartment and retrieved one of the assault rifles, checked the magazine, cocked the weapon and walked round to the front of the Kamov just as Doyle clutched in the rotor. The two crewmen were now sprinting towards the helicopter. Gunn pushed the change lever to single shot, and dropped both men at a range of 100 yards. He then climbed back into the Kamov as Doyle increased power and raised the collective stick. The Kamov lifted off the ground and climbed steadily until it was above the gorge and then Doyle edged the chopper forward until it was above the spot where they had left Tanya with Ben and Peter. Gunn went back into the passenger compartment and pulled back the sliding door.

They had no way of communicating with Tanya. Gunn knelt in the doorway of the Kamov and as it sank lower and lower he passed instructions over the intercom to Doyle at the same time hoping that Tanya and the two controllers could see him. That worked and the three of them appeared from the forest and approached the helicopter.

'Hold it there!' Gunn told Doyle as the landing wheels touched the edge of the gorge. Ben came forward first and with help from Gunn and both Tanya and Peter behind him he was dragged aboard. Peter came next and then Tanya. 'All clear,' Gunn told Doyle as he closed the door.

The Kamov climbed clear of the gorge, turned through 180° and headed east to the coast and the port of Vanino.

CHAPTER 53

Their silk-printed map and the flight charts belonging to the pilots showed that it was just over 100 miles to Vanino in a straight line of flight. Once again, Doyle had no wish to alert the Russian air traffic control or its air defence system so the Kamov flew at no more than 200 feet along the gorge followed by the river valley which curved to the south towards the coast and the port of Vanino. This increased the distance to nearly 200 miles, but with a full fuel load that posed no problem and Doyle forecast an ETA at Vanino of 2015 hours after Gunn had entered the port's coordinates into the satnav.

'That means we'll be there in daylight. Any ideas yet about an LZ for this machine?' Gunn asked.

'Open to any suggestions, buddy. I hadn't got that far yet in my plans. But the absence of Zhukov worries me. If he sent this Kamov and the five heavies to kill or capture us, what has he done?'

Tanya had put on the spare headset in the passenger compartment and joined the discussion. 'The fact that he knew...or thought he knew....that we were on the train heading for Vanino......or that other place....'

'Sovetskaya Gavan,' Doyle provided.

'Yes, that place........to me means that somehow he knew we weren't on the Tynda train. How, I've no idea, but in this part of Russia I expect he's got spies and informers everywhere who have been paid well to provide him with information.'

'Unfortunately, I reckon you right and continuing our policy of worst case planning that means that he's waiting for us.....or a call which he won't get from this helicopter to tell him that we've either been killed or captured,' Gunn offered.

'Presumably he got to Sovetskaya Gavan in his Gulfstream and has landed at the airport which Langley told us about,' Tanya continued.

'Yuzhno-Sakhalinsk.'

'Whatever....how many passengers can a Gulfstream carry?' Tanya asked.

'Ask the guys in back with you if he told them what model he had, as the Gulfstream series varies from a twin turbo-prop with about 25 seats through a twin jet with the same number of seats down to a single prop 4 seater.'

'Wait.........Ben says he spoke of a Gulfstream Commander....any help?'

'Yea, twin engine with seating for no more than eight pax.'

'So what's the plan then? It won't be long before he realises that blocking the track has failed.'

'It seems to me,' Gunn joined the conversation, 'that unless we land this chopper well away from Vanino, Zhukov will know of our arrival. I expect he's in his Gulfstream and at the airport. Therefore our first step must be to avoid the airport and land this machine where he won't hear it arrive. That'll mean a walk to the port or a bus or taxi ride. We've got plenty of time and Ben says he has no problem with walking. Any objections so far?'

'Wait.......I'll ask the guys back here,' Tanya answered. And then replied, 'no objections from your passengers.'

'OK John, can you check the charts and give me a new course which avoids the airport and.....with luck, gives us an LZ.'

'OK,' and Gunn pulled the chart onto his lap. 'The airport is well to the north of both Vanino and Sovetskaya Gavan. The airport lies in what looks like a coastal plain. Between that plain and Vanino there are two fairly substantial re-entrants which will act as useful baffles to muffle the sound of this chopper. I'm going to give you directions shortly into a re-entrant that runs all the way to the coast and with the prevailing wind coming off the sea from the east I very much doubt if anyone at the airport will hear us. And if you hug the deck, the airport ground and air surveillance radar won't see us.'

'Got that....you just give me directions and I'll give you a demonstration of hugging the deck!' Doyle boasted.

They flew on for another half hour in the Tumnin River valley and then Gunn gave him fresh directions.

'I want you to go into the next valley on our starboard side. Stay as low as possible over the crest of the ridge on our right as this is the only time that we could be spotted by radar. Once over the crest drop right down to the valley floor and give us your demonstration of deck hugging. OK?'

'Roger to that...here we go,' and Doyle took the Kamov helicopter over the ridge through a natural ride in the taiga barely feet above the undergrowth and then dropped down into the valley.

'Now, this valley should go all the way to the Tumnin Estuary and the port. It's less than 50 miles to the port so we should be there in about twenty minutes.'

'What we want is an open space - like a car park - where we can dump the chopper and get away from it before it attracts attention from the local police,' was Doyle's comment as he manoeuvred the chopper at 'daisy cutting' height along the valley.

CHAPTER 54

Minute by minute the scenery below.....'but only just below them,' Gunn winced as Doyle flew round a small farm building....began to change. Gone were the miles of wild taiga forest to be replaced firstly by small farm houses with just an acre or two of cultivated land and then larger farms and finally streets and housing estates.

They were so low that there was only a limited view of what lay ahead, but in the distance they could see the river estuary opening out with the container port on the south side. And then an almost tailor-made LZ was offered to them. Within the port perimeter was a container park....hundreds of containers all stacked ready for loading onto ships or transporters to take them into the Russian hinterland.

'That's it buddy!' Doyle exclaimed. 'That square gap amongst the containers. If I put the chopper down there it'll be ages before they find it....well, at least a few minutes by which time we'll be well away.'

The Kamov skimmed over a road and the perimeter fence of the port area and dropped into the slot which Doyle had spotted. The wheels had hardly touched the ground than Tanya had the sliding door open and she and Peter helped Ben out. They were joined by Gunn and Doyle and the five disappeared amongst the containers before the Kamov's rotors had stopped turning.

'I think I spotted Berth 4 just before we landed,' Gunn said, leading the way through the container park towards the dock area. 'Now all we have to do is avoid any port officials or guards until we reach the 'Unsongia' container ship.'

Berth 4 was at the far end of the dock. The container ship in that berth was flying the South Korean flag with its circular red and blue Yin-Yang symbol surrounded by short black 'kwae' bars. The container port was busy, but no one took any notice of the five people weaving their way through the usual dockside clutter of vehicles and equipment. They reached the gangway which led up the side of the ship. Gunn paused and turned. There was no sign of Tanya who had been bringing up the rear.

'What happened to Tanya?'

'She said to carry on and she'd catch up with us,' Peter said.

Gunn looked at his watch. 'We've got four hours until the ship sails. Be ready for surprises guys, I just can't believe we've been so lucky to avoid Zhukov.'

The four men reached the deck and made their way to the high, elevated sterncastle. They climbed up successive flights of companionway stairs until they reached the bridge. Gunn glanced back. There was still no sign of Tanya. The absence of any crew on the 'Unsongia' was unusual to say the least. Gunn drew the Glock from his shoulder holster and tried the door into the bridge. It opened.

'Good evening........Mr Gunn I presume and Mr Barnes.'

Both Gunn and Doyle spun round, but as they did so, armed men surrounded them. Facing them was Zhukov.....large, shaven head, pierced ears and plug ugly......it had to be Zhukov.

'But no Tanya......' Zhukov continued, 'what a shame I had to dispose of her in Khabarovsk. No doubt you will tell me what happened to Georgy Balashov.'

Gunn and Doyle were efficiently disarmed by Zhukov's men and Ben and Peter were pushed into the bridge.

'What's happened to the Captain of this ship?' Gunn asked, mentally kicking himself for walking straight into the trap set by Zhukov. 'And did Zhukov really believe that Tanya had been killed at the station by Balashov?' Gunn wondered.

'You really do underrate me Mr Gunn. Once I learned that you were on an eastbound train to the coast, it was not difficult to guess that you would make for a ship. This ship is the only one due to sail tonight and after some persuasion.....yes I did have to execute one of his officers......the Captain told me that he expected you to join the ship this evening. I'm rather hoping that you have returned my helicopter, but enough of that. I have decided that I do not want to involve my organisation in an exchange of agents so that means that it just remains for me to dispose of the four of you.'

CHAPTER 55

When Zhukov had sprung his trap there had been four armed men concealed outside the bridge. Two of them had come in behind Gunn, Doyle, Peter and Ben and were now covering them with what looked to Gunn like PP-90M1 machine pistols - each magazine holding 32 rounds of 9mm ammunition. Zhukov appeared to be unarmed except for the blood-stained machete lying on the chart table beside him - no doubt used to execute the crewman of the 'Unsongia'. Zhukov's men had removed both of his Glocks - the 17 which he'd been holding and the 26 from his ankle holster. This rapid assessment of their desperate situation took but split seconds in Gunn's mind as he realised how hopeless any attempt to overpower the armed men would be. It would certainly result in at least one of them being killed.

'What the hell had happened to Tanya?' Gunn wondered.

As if in reply to his unspoken query, there were two rapid, muffled coughs behind him from the direction of the door into the bridge from the companionway outside. Out of the corner of his eye, Gunn saw both armed men sink to the floor. This triggered a bedlam of activity. Doyle ripped a machine pistol out of the grasp of the man nearest him and fired off half a magazine in the direction of Zhukov who had thrown himself onto the floor behind the chart table. Gunn saw his hand appear over the edge of the table reaching for his machete. He dived across the chart table, snatching the machete out of Zhukov's grasp and fell to the floor beside him. Zhukov screamed with rage and threw himself at

Gunn. Holding the machete with both hands, Gunn swung at Zhukov's snarling shaven head with all his strength. The two-handed blow was delivered with all Gunn's upper-body strength and would certainly have a driven a tee shot a clear 300 yards. In this case it removed Zhukov's head as cleanly as a knife slicing the top off a breakfast boiled egg.

Doyle peered over the edge of the chart table at his bloodied accomplice on the floor.

'You OK, buddy?'

'Yea, I'm fine,' and Gunn got to his feet. Where's our saviour?'

'She's gone off to release the Captain and his crew.'

'Are there any more of Zhukov's men?'

'No.....Tanya shot two of them outside the bridge using the silencer on her Smith and Wesson and then the two inside the bridge. There are probably another two – the pilots - up at the airport. Ah! here she is,' and Tanya reappeared with the South Korean Captain of the 'Unsongia'.

Gunn went over and gave Tanya a hug.

'Yuk!' was her response to his blood-spattered hug, before she went over to inspect the headless body of Zhukov. 'Poetic justice I think.'

CHAPTER 56

The container ship 'Unsongia' sailed at 2330 hours, minus one crew member, but with five passengers. Once the ship had reached international waters, a Blackhawk helicopter from the US 7th Fleet's carrier 'USS Enterprise' landed on top of the stacked containers and lifted off the five passengers. The same helicopter dropped them at Hong Kong's Kai Tak international airport two days later. From there Gunn, Tanya and Ben caught the British Airways flight to London. One hour later, Doyle and Peter caught the American Airlines flight to Washington via Los Angeles.

*

'Come in,' Miles Thompson, the Head of BID invited Gunn, Tanya and Ben into his office. 'Grab a chair and help yourself to coffee.' Miles joined his three employees. 'I won't keep you long, but thought you might like to know what we've done to try and help the North Koreans in that gulag.' His audience all nodded. 'Both the US President and our Prime Minister have received assurances from the Russian Prime Minister that he will accept a visit by officials from the United Nations High Commission for Refugees to resolve the problem of what is to be done with the 5,000 North Koreans in that gulag which you discovered. He has promised that they will not be sent back to North Korea. Let's hope he will keep that promise. The Russian Prime Minister claims to have no knowledge of the existence of that particular gulag although he refused to acknowledge the existence of any other gulags.'

'A joint effort by our CE Directorate and the FBI has identified and.......I think the appropriate term would be 'neutralised'.......the KKS sleepers and branches of Faraway Travel in conjunction with other European counter-intelligence agencies. Intriguing as it may have seemed at the time, there is no further evidence to corroborate the conspiracy theory of the survival of the passengers of Flight KAL 007. So that will have to remain a mystery for someone else to solve.'

'Now, Ben, as I haven't appointed a replacement yet for Rayner, I am still the Head of the Espionage Directorate and therefore have approved David Simpson's suggestion that you take a fortnight's convalescent leave. I know that your sailing was interrupted John, but I shall expect you to rejoin your Russian language course on Monday. Mike Dimmock has an assignment in Japan for you Tanya, but like John, that can wait until Monday.'

*

Sarah Cooper emerged from Spiridon's souvenir shop and rejoined her husband, Matthew, for a coffee and sticky cake at a pavement restaurant on Yeltsin Ulitsa in Tynda. The couple from New York were on a package tour which included a two day stopover at the city at the junction of the Baikal Amur Railway and the Trans Siberian Railway.

'Find anything?' Matthew asked through a mouthful of cake.

'Only these Babushka dolls,' Sarah admitted placing the little wooden dolls on the table. 'Got to talking with the woman who served me. You remember that jumbo jet shot down by the Soviets back in the eighties?'

'Yea, a South Korean 747 on a flight from Alaska to Seoul. All the passengers were killed.'

'She says that none of the passengers were killed and those that are still alive are living in various parts of Russia. She said some are living in this city.'

'Yea, well some say that 9/11 was a US Government plot to justify the invasion of Iraq. The World is full of nutters, honey,' and Matthew stuffed the remainder of the cake into his mouth.

'I don't know, Matt. She sounded very convincing. Do you think she was trying to get a message to the US Government?'

'Maybe honey.......now where are we going to have lunch?' her husband asked finishing off the crumbs of the cake.

OTHER BOOKS FEATURING JOHN GUNN

BY BRIAN NICHOLSON

GWEILO

The theft of a birthright has been the motive for murder since Jacob usurped it from his elder brother Esau. The loss of the birthright to the immense riches of Hong Kong leads to a plot by two men, one Chinese and the other a 'gweilo' - a descendant of the first settlers to arrive in Hong Kong. The catastrophic meltdown of the Chernobyl nuclear power station provides the solution - the destruction of Hong Kong rather than hand it back to the China. Fluent in both Cantonese and Mandarin Chinese, John Gunn is recruited for this assignment by the British Intelligence Directorate. But the countdown to this nuclear holocaust has already begun.

AL SAMAK

This is a rocket-paced thriller about a conspiracy by die-hard communists to sell nuclear warheads to Saddam Hussein. The conspirators are led by an ex-KGB psychopath whose bloodthirsty brutality even sickened the KGB and the Soviet leadership. Their choice of arms dealer is Hassan Hussein whose Kurdish village has been destroyed by Saddam's chemical gas attack. Horribly disfigured by the gas attack, Hassan has his own plans for the nuclear warheads. This is John Gunn's second assignment with the British Intelligence Directorate. It's a story of intrigue, treachery, revenge and unbelievable violence during the summer of 2002 when the USA, UK and IAEA were searching for the 'smoking gun' to justify the invasion of Iraq.

ASHANTI GOLD

The priceless ingots of Ashanti Gold are secured in the vaults of the Bank of Ghana. Gold will buy weapons and weapons are needed by the West African exiles, ruthless arms dealers, corrupt diplomats and politicians on both sides of the Atlantic conspiring to overthrow the governments of all West African countries. This is John Gunn's third assignment with the British Intelligence Directorate which has sent him to Ghana to investigate the disappearance of an SIS agent from the British High Commission.

FIRE DRAGON

Colliding tectonic plates, erupting volcanoes, earthquakes and tsunamis make Indonesia the most volatile geological archipelago in the World. This explosively unstable geology is matched by the volatile conspiracy of Romano Rusman who is determined to return Indonesia to a communist dictatorship. He has stumbled on the vast treasure hidden by Admiral Yamamoto at the end of World War 2 and uses this limitless source of funding to conspire with North Korea to place its nuclear weapons in space orbit out of the reach of the IAEA inspections and US spy satellites. A fatal error occurs while the nuclear warheads are being shipped from North Korea to Indonesia, which results in John Gunn's fourth assignment with the British Intelligence Directorate and his confrontation with man-eating komodo dragons in the 'ring of fire'.

CALYPSO

How can five yachts disappear without trace on a Caribbean cruise? What has happened to the British Warship sent to investigate? Where are Iraq's chemical weapons? Why is London lobbying for the release of a Camp Delta prisoner and why has a WW2 Dakota been shipped to the UK from the Mojave Desert? John Gunn is pitched into a desperate race against time on this assignment for the British Intelligence Directorate, as the answers to these questions reveal a conspiracy for a catastrophic terrorist atrocity in London.

SHARK

What is the secret that lies buried in the sand of the Iraqi Desert and why has this led to the murder of a British Intelligence agent? What was the name the gunman tried to utter before he died? Who is blackmailing senior members of the Cabinet Office and Intelligence Services? Who was the eighth man and who is the mole crippling the British Intelligence Directorate? Desperate urgency is needed to answer these questions because the next agent to be murdered is John Gunn.

TRAITOR

The spectre of a traitor who betrayed fellow soldiers in a Japanese POW camp in Hong Kong has risen from the grave to haunt the British Intelligence Directorate. A deliberate hit-and-run murder in London of the son of an ex-POW is followed by the murder of an agent during a break-in at Gunn's London house to search for war crime papers and diaries relating to the betrayal in 1941. Twice Gunn escapes the 21st Century Samurai warriors from a proscribed Japanese Mafia cult thought to have been responsible for the Sarin gas attack on the Tokyo subway.

Every effort is made by both the Director of the British Intelligence Directorate and the Japanese Mafia to prevent him taking over the investigation. This turns Gunn into a fugitive from the British police and the Counter-Espionage Department of BID as his search inevitably leads him back to Japan.

ASSASSIN

Decapitated and mutilated cadavers are discovered in the USA, UK, Sweden and Belgium. The MO in each incident is identical. The victims are linked by a package tour to Russia. Three members of that tour are still alive....but for how long? And what is the connection to KAL Flight 007 shot down by the Soviet Union in 1983?

The British Intelligence Directorate and the CIA are pitched into a race to save the survivors of the package tour and expose double agents in their own intelligence organisations.

This latest assignment for BID agents John Gunn and Tanya Kazakova and the CIA's Doyle Barnes takes them into the bleak forest wilderness of the Russian Taiga.

THE AUTHOR

Excitement started at an early age for the author; returning from India with his family in June 1945, aged 3, the ship in which the family was embarked was chased by a Japanese submarine which fortunately had run out of torpedoes. Brian Nicholson had an equally exciting career in the army for 35 years of which the last 10 were spent working with the officers of the Secret Intelligence Service in various overseas appointments in Hong Kong, Ghana and Indonesia.

He was made an OBE in 1985 and received a Commendation from the Commander British Forces Hong Kong in 1987 for his success in the negotiations with the Chinese Government on the handover of Hong Kong. At the request of the Royal Navy Funeral Department, while he was Defence Attaché in Jakarta, he solved the mystery of what happened to Sub-Lieutenant Gregor Riggs. Riggs was the last of the 23 Commandoes on the ill-fated Australian Commando raid, Operation Rimau, on Japanese shipping in Singapore Harbour in World War 2. The author discovered the remains of the young officer on a remote island in the Indonesian Archipelago and returned them to the family for burial with full military honours at the Changi Military Cemetery in Singapore.

In 1990, as Military Advisor to Jerry Rawlings, Ghana's President, he was directed to plan the successful West African military intervention in Liberia after the horrific videoed torture and assassination of the country's despotic dictator, Master Sergeant Samuel Doe. These are but a few of the exciting experiences in a colourful career which formed the backdrop to the eight books which he has written. He is currently researching his ninth book. Brian Nicholson is married with two adult daughters and lives in Richmond where his time is taken up with writing, golf, shooting and sailing.

THE AUTHOR

BRIAN NICHOLSON

Lightning Source UK Ltd.
Milton Keynes UK
UKOW04n2053260717
306106UK00001B/1/P